7. Lu 14, 1997

MW01286592

*We know the ghosts
to the ghosts some idea
will give tell more ghosts.
help with love
Mom Dad.*

*Printed
For
Quixote Press
by*
BRENNAN PRINTING
*100 Main Street
Deep River, Iowa 52222*
515-595-2000

GHOSTLY TALES
OF
SOUTHWEST MINNESOTA

by

Ruth D. Hein

Cover Design by
Bobbi Douglas (Prickett)

Copyright © 1989 Ruth D. Hein

QUIXOTE PRESS
R.R. #4, Box 33B
Blvd. Station
Sioux City, Iowa 51109

i

© 1989 by Ruth D. Hein

* * * * * * * * * *

Although the author has exhaustively researched all sources to ensure the accuracy and completeness of the information contained in this book, she assumes no responsibility for errors, inaccuracies, omissions, or any inconsistency herein. Any slights of people or organizations are unintentional. Readers should consult an attorney or accountant for specific applications to their individual publishing ventures.

QUIXOTE
PRESS
Bruce Carlson
R.R. #4, Box 33B
Blvd. Station
Sioux City, Iowa
51109

PRINTED
IN
U.S.A.

This Book Is Dedicated To

my husband Ken

and our four children:
Pat Wangberg
Mike Hein
Ted Hein
Dea Klumper
and their families

who all let me become,
for a while,
"the ghost story lady."

Ruth D. Hein

TABLE OF CONTENTS

PREFACE

In trying for a variety of ghostly tales representative of Southwest Minnesota, I found one from pioneer times, one from the days of the Underground Railroad, and some set in historic or abandoned buildings, ghost towns, and cemeteries.

Other tales came from the lives of individuals and their families. There are some stories from the long-ago days, but others are contemporary ghosts.

If people who had ghost stories were not willing to let me use them, I didn't. If some told me their stories but preferred anonymity, I respected that wish by using different names.

There are more ghosts lurking in this area than I could fit into this book. I hope someone will record them before they are forgotten.

ACKNOWLEDGMENTS

I wish to thank all who responded to my request for leads. Their help made the book possible.

Local historians and personnel from county historical societies were also helpful. Writing the book would have been much more difficult without their assistance.

Other resources were the staff and references at Nobles County Library and Information Center and several area newspaper staff members and the articles they provided. All were truly appreciated.

I also wish to thank all my friends who listened to and answered my many questions and then left me time to gather and write the stories. They are true friends!

Thanks also to the publisher, Bruce Carlson of Quixote Press. We agreed that I would write this second book of ghost stores after I co-authored the first book, *Ghostly Tales of Northeast Iowa*, in 1988.

Ruth D. Hein
Worthington, Minnesota

I know not who these mute folk are
   Who share the unlit place with me--
   Those stones out under the low-limbed tree
Doubtless bear names that the mosses mar.

--From "Ghost House"
by Robert Frost

The reader must appreciate the fact that none of these stories have ever been published before. Some of them could cause embarrassment to people living today. Because of that, some of the stories use fictitious names. In those cases, it should be understood that any similarity between those names and actual people, living or dead, is purely coincidental.

"...AND YOU WILL FIND MY BODY..."

 innesota. The land of 10,000 lakes. The land of the Dahkotas. The land of the sky-tinted water. Birthplace of many rivers flowing in all directions. Land of prairie, forest, bluff, and waterfall.

Edward D. Neill used such phrases to describe this state, in his *History of Minnesota*. Minnesota, where 70 persons died in the blizzard of 1873.

Southwest Minnesota. The "dark days," "the calamitous days." Land of grasshopper invasions, land of fierce blizzards, according to Arthur P. Rose's *An Illustrated History of Nobles County, Minnesota* (1908). Nobles County, where four persons died in the blizzard of 1873.

That was a terrible storm, recorded at Fort Snelling as the most violent in the Northwest for 50 years. The temperature stayed at about 18 *below* 0 during all three days of the storm.

John Weston was one of the four victims who died in Nobles County. He was a farmer in Seward

(13)

Township which is in the northern part of the county and just west of Graham Lakes Township.

On the morning of January 7, Weston left for Graham Lakes to get a load of wood. It was a beautiful morning for early January. Most of the  farmers either went to visit their neighbors or left for town for flour or some other necessity. On his way home, although the day had started out clear and mild, Weston was caught in the storm that came around noon like a great white wall from the Northwest.

Trying to get home, he missed his house even though he drove his sled and oxen across his own land, as the tracks showed later. He circled twice, then went more northward, back into Graham Lakes Township. There, Rose's history tells it, he "unhitched and abandoned his ox team, and the animals, after wandering a while, turned the yoke and choked to death. They were found later on the bank of Jack Creek."

Apparently Weston then walked *with* the storm, toward Hersey (now Brewster, a town just a few miles south of Graham Lakes and about eight miles northeast of Worthington).

After he walked about 12 miles, Weston fell on his face in the snow and long grass. But, of course, that wasn't immediately known.

The storm was so severe for three days that searchers had to wait for it to die down. When they could finally safely look for John Weston, they found the sled and oxen but went home toward evening without finding their owner.

The next April, after the snow had melted, another search party was successful in finding the body.

So far, the story is history recorded in several published references. But it is also a well-known ghost story, retold by A.P. Miller in *The Worthington Advance* of January 13, 1881, eight years after the blizzard.

A D.J. Cosper, a good friend of Weston's, had been a member of the first search party. The group hadn't found Weston, and they went back home. Later that day, Cosper was feeding his livestock. He came out of the stable to get water for his horses. About half way down the slope to the well, he saw John Weston coming up the path from the creek. It was so natural he didn't think a thing about it at first. Weston was wearing his blue soldier's overcoat he usually wore in cold weather. He greeted Cosper as usual with, "How goes it?"

Cosper's answer was, "Why, Weston, I thought you were frozen to death!"

Weston answered, "I am, and you will find my body a mile and a half northwest of Hersey." Then he was gone.

After a while, as Mr. Cosper went on about his chores, he realized he had seen a ghost. He told the story to others, and people believed he told the truth. There was no reason to make up such a story about his long-time friend.

But this is really a *double* ghost story. Weston's ghost also appeared to his wife. Mary Weston told it this way:

"On the second night of the storm, I heard a knock at the door. I dozed off again. Then I heard a second knock. Over the noise of the wind and the sifting snow, I shouted, 'What do you want?' Someone said, 'Did you know that John was frozen to death?' The voice sounded like my brother's. Our son heard it, too, and said from his bed, 'Mother, did Uncle say Pa was frozen to death?' "

Mrs. Weston went to the door then, but no one

was out there and she found no fresh tracks in the snow. When others checked with her brother, a Mr. Linderman, he said he had not been at the Weston home that night. Those who heard Mary's story thought that John Weston wanted to let his family know of his death without frightening his wife, so he made his plight known through the voice of his brother-in-law.

As recorded, the rest of the story is that when the snow melted in April, 1873, John Weston's body *was* found, just where his ghost said he would be – a mile and a half northwest of Hersey, near a slough, where the snow had been deep for those three long months.

A PROTECTIVE SPIRIT

 omething unusual happened a few years ago in an old farmhouse near St. Peter. The woman who told this story has moved to another state, but she's still wondering about the incident.

She said, "I think there is a good spirit walking the earth who can be credited with saving my life!"

Janeen went on to tell what had happened to her. "I was going down the stairs to the main floor one night," she said, "when I started to trip. At the same time, it seemed as if something or someone gently brushed by me and said, 'That's what happened to me.' Yet it was more a thought or a mind message, not a definite audible voice. But it turned out all right. A little scary, but okay because I was okay.

(19)

"I didn't think twice about it, until the next day when I was telling my fourteen-year-old daughter Trish about it. Trish listened at first, then looked as if she were about to interrupt. I said, 'What?' and Trish said, 'Mom, this is really weird! The very same thing happened to me, a while back. It was sort of scary, and I didn't tell anyone. I was afraid you'd think I was making it up. But it made me wonder if something unearthly would happen to one of us.'

"I asked Trish to tell me exactly what had happened. She told me, 'I was going downstairs one night, a couple of weeks ago. It was so hot in my room that night! I started down for a glass of cold milk. Just about halfway down, someone or something went by me, but didn't say anything. I had the feeling it was a woman, but it wasn't you or Sandi or anyone I know.' "

Both mother and daughter kept these occurrences in mind, without saying anything to anyone else. About two years later, Janeen was having trouble with hemorrhaging and this naturally worried her. One afternoon about four o'clock, she called her doctor, who said he was about to leave his office. But he listened, asked a few questions, and ended the conversation with, "Call me if you have more trouble."

That night, not long before midnight, Janeen woke up to see a woman standing in the doorway of her room. "It wasn't either of the girls. She looked older. She stood there framed by the doorway in a filmy, flowing gown. She was

(20)

beckoning to me. She wasn't talking but just stretching out a hand and arm toward me, motioning me to get out of bed and come to her. I didn't feel like getting up, but the woman kept on coaxing me to, until I actually did get out of bed more out of curiosity than anything.

"As soon as I did, my concern was for myself and my condition. I realized I was hemorrhaging badly. I forgot all about the ghost or spirit or whatever had been compelling me to get up."

Today Janeen says, "I didn't know then what it was all about, but if that hadn't happened – and if I hadn't gotten up to see who or what she was – I wouldn't have known how serious the hemorrhaging was.

"I called the doctor again," she continued. "Then Sandi drove me to the hospital where I got the help I needed, and my condition improved."

The next time the three discussed the incidents on the stairs and in Janeen's bedroom, they realized that there was a ghost in their home. They had accepted her by then as a good ghost. She was, in their opinion, the spirit of a woman who had long ago tripped on the stairs and who had come back to protect the later occupants, at least the women, from falling all the way down the stairs or in any other way ending their time on earth prematurely.

This is what she must have meant with her message, "That's what happened to me."

A GHOST CAUSES AN ACCIDENT

ome people have creepy feelings when they're in a cemetery. Others are very quiet and reflective when they walk through one.

Some young people have been known to vandalize graveyards. They tip over the loose headstones – those tall, old ones not yet cemented to a heavy, broader base in the earth. Adults, on the other hand, are often seen searching the records on the markers, seeking out some historical or genealogical detail.

As a youngster driving by a cemetery with my family, in Dad's old green '28 Chevy, I've been known to make the dry remark, "This is sure a dead part of town." In fact, it was a game with us kids to see who could say it first.

Poets have observed that the cemetery really belongs to the dead, as in Kenneth Fearing's "Thirteen O'clock" where the buried ones say, "Go away, live people, stop haunting the dead."

In the story "Over the Fence and Out" in the recent

paperback *Ghostly Tales of Northeast Iowa*, a young boy is badly scared by a three-eyed ghost in a cemetery. Or were his older brothers and their friend playing a prank on Robbie?

But I have never heard of an adult being as frightened by a cemetery incident as the woman was who told this story.

"It happened in Cottonwood County," she said, "at a cemetery real close to the road." Then she brought a local character into it.

"Everyone for miles around knew unpredictable old Hank, who had lived there all his life. Everyone had read about him in the papers when he'd killed himself several years earlier. That was a well-known fact.

"Everyone knew, too, that he'd been buried in that cemetery along the main drag.

"Don't ask me what I was thinking about that day. I just don't know. But as I drove past the cemetery in broad daylight, something made me glance up.

"There was old Hank, leaning against a tree. He was staring at the inscription on one of those huge, white bronze monuments in the part where all the older graves are, down along the road fence.

"I knew Hank had been dead a while. But there he was! As I tried to cope, my mind did a flip-flop and so did my car.

"I was so scared that I let go of the steering wheel and my car went in the ditch. When I came to, Hank was gone. Don't think I didn't have a hard time explaining why my car was in the ditch!"

MORE THAN A ROCKING CHAIR?

 couple and their seven children, ages twelve on down, moved to a rambling farmplace south of Ortonville. In the living room of the two-story house, they found an old wicker rocking chair that had been left by previous occupants. Only that. They thought

about throwing it out, but there was something comfortable about its look. It belonged. Otherwise, the family had furnished the house themselves, bringing with them enough of everything to fill the old ten-room frame structure.

The first day was a busy one, but the children found time to explore each room on the main floor, all five bedrooms upstairs, and (on the pretense

of needing to carry down the fruit jars and crocks) even the basement. By evening, they were tired as were their parents. All went up to bed at the same time. A few beds still had to be made up, and the oldest ones helped.

From that first night in the house on, as soon as the family had all gone to bed, they would hear the rocking chair sigh and squeak as it rocked in its corner downstairs. It always happened just as soon as the lights were out and each family member was cozily settled in bed.

Whenever anyone jumped out of bed and ran down-stairs to see what was hap-pening, the chair was still; the rocking had stopped. it was just an old chair rocking, after all. But the children found them-selves wishing their stairway had a banister. It

would be more fun to *slide* down to check on the chair, and they thought they could get there faster, too, before the thing that caused the rocking made itself invisible.

What made the chair rock remained a mystery. And later the mother had a strange experience in the same house. She was coming up one day from the dimly lighted basement when she plainly felt a hand resting on her shoulder. Briefly. Lightly. Almost like a loving, comforting touch. This was rather bewildering, as she was sure her husband was at work in the farthest field and the children were all in school.

She hurried on up the steps. She looked around. But nothing was there. No one else was in the house at the time. At least, no other mortal.

HERMAN AND MAUDE

 onnie Jordahl remembers the Palace Theater in Luverne in its early years. "My mother sold tickets there," she said. "And my father was a projectionist. My sister and I ushered. Oh, but that was a long time ago!"

Yes, it was. The Palace Theater at Main and Freeman in Luverne is one of the town's many buildings that reflect the early years of Luverne and Rock County. Some have been restored and are on the National Register of Historic Places, as is the Palace.

This year, the pipe organ that was installed in 1926 in the Palace is being repaired.

"When the workers are finished," Bonnie revealed, "we plan to hold recitals in the theater. Maybe we can also have an old-fashioned silent movie, with organ accompaniment. If that works out, we hope to have it in connection with an 'Open House.' It's also possible that the old ballroom in the building will become a museum. If it does, it will be open during the summers."

The idea for musical accompaniment to silent movies reflects the long ago days in the Palace, about which some ghost stories have circulated.

Among the known facts are these: the beautiful new Palace Theater was built in 1915 by Herman Jochims, the local theater manager, at a cost of $50,000. It was opened for use on September 29, 1915.

Four years later, Herman married Maude. Maude played piano and later the pipe organ, to accompany silent movies shown in the theater.

Since the early years, the theater has been used for traveling shows, operatic and dramatic productions, and modern movies *with* sound.

From time to time, when the building is in use, a story about the presence of a ghost surfaces. People in the audience and ushers in the aisles say they have seen the ghost of Herman Jochims. His favorite place seems to be the balcony; from there he can keep an eye on what's going on and how his theater is being used.

And he can be close to Maude as he looks down from the balcony to the orchestra pit in front of the stage. It is said that Maude also returns to her old place at the organ.

Perhaps the couple, by their ghostly presence, hope to keep control over what happens there. It could be that Herman and Maude are responsible for objects being moved or broken or lost. Imagine how an actor felt when the prop he was to pick up from a coffee table at the beginning of Act III was simply not there. Yet it *had* been there at dress rehearsal the night before and every rehearsal before that!

Herman probably likes to sit in the balcony and listen to his Maude play the organ. Currently, while it is under repair, no musical accompaniment is planned for any production. But Maude still somehow provides music every now and then.

"Maude may have had a hard time making the break," one Luverne resident offered. "She was so used to sitting there. When she accompanied the old movies, she played beautifully. Now there's usually no one in the pit area, especially in the middle of the night. But folks claim they can still hear the music. Mostly those who leave late at night after a practice. And the janitors, too, when they check the building after everyone's gone."

One night custodian was overheard in the lobby. "It was classical music," he declared. "I've heard it more than once. And it's weird to hear it at midnight when you're turning out the lights and you know you're the last one in the building. One night it was like someone was there turning out the lights ahead of me.

"No one ever hangs around here long, and neither do I. I check all the rooms and finish locking up, and I get

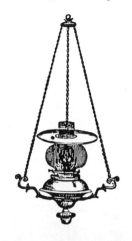

out of here as fast as I can. In fact, if you have any questions, save them. I'm out of here!"

When the organ is repaired, will Maude come back to the Palace Theater to play it? Will she be one of the guests at the "Open House"? If the old ballroom becomes a museum, will visitors see Maude and Herman waltzing together as in the early years?

TUNED IN?

ome events in life seem to defy logical explanation. Yet the events themselves are interesting, and the uncanny ways they occur and catch our attention lead to intriguing questions and speculation. We find ourselves trying to figure out the connections.

Are some individuals endowed with special powers? For example, do they have such a keen awareness that they can perceive danger to loved ones, even at a distance, at the very moment it appears? Is it possible to be "tuned in" somehow to what will happen?

Could a person hear the ticking of a clock (when there is no clock around) and know it foretells the ticking away of life's moments?

Such, at least, was the experience of a family in one of the border counties of Southwest Minnesota. Berniece was the person who seemed to be "tuned in," and at a young age. When Berniece was thirteen, she sat by the bedside of her father who lay dying of cancer. She had been told he would not recover, and she spent as much time with him as she could. "I wanted to be with him every moment," she said later. "I loved him very much."

"For his last two days," Berniece continued, "he was incoherent. But when he did open his eyes now and then, I felt that he saw me or Mom or whoever was there.

"One day in the dead quiet of his room, I heard a ticking sound coming from one corner. His old alarm clock wasn't on the dresser any more, almost

as if no one wanted to remind him of time passing. Yet there was the ticking. I was mystified. I had heard of the insect called the deathwatch, a small European wood-boring beetle. It makes a ticking sound that is thought to be an omen of death. I kept wondering about that sound.

"I was soon aware that each person who came into the room also heard it. It was as though there was an invisible clock in the room, and it seemed to all of us that it was marking off Dad's last moments.

"At the instant of his death, I was sitting there by him, still holding his hand. Dad opened his eyes and looked at me. Then he was gone. At the same time that I heard what my Mom called the death rattle, the ticking stopped.

"Did the ticking signal Dad's approaching death? Some of the relatives thought it was a spiritualistic experience. Others felt it was more like a death rap, a sign. There *was* a sign – the ticking. And when death came, it stopped."

Berniece told of another incident. Her husband Jim was born and grew up in Southwest Minnesota. When he was a young boy, not many doctors practiced out of their homes or in offices in small towns. And it was hard to get a doctor to come on a house call from the  larger towns like the county seats, especially at night and during a winter storm.

"One stormy night," Berniece said, "Jim's brother, who was seven, took suddenly ill. Later, his family realized he'd had an appendicitis attack. Complications set in and the boy died in his mother's arms before morning.

"The family became aware that night that the front door had opened though none of them had opened it. They were sure it had been locked toward evening. There was no reason to unlock it because the doctor couldn't get there and no one else was expected. They felt it was a sign, but they never really understood how it happened. Any more than they understood why the old violin, stored in its case in the attic, began to play tune after tune."

Could there have been a good spirit in the house? One that wanted to warn the family of the impending death? or wanted to somehow compel the doctor to come and help the boy? or comfort the bereaved with the violin music?

There was nothing unusual about what Berniece herself was doing one day about thirty years ago. Yet she remembers so clearly, just as if she were watching a movie or a tape of more recent events. She said, "I was standing at the kitchen sink, scrubbing some new garden potatoes to cook for supper. Suddenly I heard my daughter scream out, 'Mommy!' "

Even though thirteen-year old Linda was spending a few days with her cousins on their farm about ten miles away, Berniece searched for her. "I was so taken by the realness of her scream that I hunted all through our big three-story house, calling out her name and expecting an answer. But none came. I even went outside and walked all the way around the house and yard, listening for her and wondering if she could have come home without my knowing it. But she was nowhere in sight.

"I got more scared or the minutes passed. Something seemed to be telling me she'd been hurt or maybe even killed, and I had a strange feeling that her ghost had come to warn me. I tried to shrug off the thought and get on with the day.

"About an hour later, I went shopping for groceries. I couldn't decide which brand of cereal to buy. I didn't really have my mind on what I was doing. But I was trying to be objective and not be persuaded by what came free in the package when the manager came over to me. But not to solve my problem. He said, 'Bernie, someone's here to see you. Come this way with me, please.'

"My thoughts raced to the scream I'd heard. Something *had* happened to Linnie. I was sure, now.

"And there, at the front entrance, stood my distraught sister-in-law. She said, 'I have Linnie in the car. You might want to take her to the Doc for stitches. She has a nasty cut on her head.'

"As we hurried to her car, she told me what had happened. 'Linda and Jason were taking lunch out to the field to Mike. He was working less than half a mile from the house, but the kids got thrown off the horse.'

"I asked her how long ago. She said, 'At 11:30.' And that was the exact same time I'd heard Linda scream out, 'Mommy!' Eerie? You bet!"

(41)

A CREEPY COINCIDENCE

peaking of cemeteries, some are cheerful places peaceably laid out in the open, warmed by the sun, and brightened by colorful blooming plants or artifical wreaths. Others are creepy and dark, their markers lying helter-skelter in the shadows of many trees and shrubs and overgrown with tangled grass and weeds.

Of the latter type, there was one on a hill outside of St. Peter. It was so thick with vegetation that no caretaker mowed any more. The undergrowth seemed determined to crowd out or hide the dead. If this verdant hilltop burial place wasn't called Green Cemetery, it should have been.

A young woman tells of a time when she was a teenager, when she and two friends explored that gloomy cemetery late one August day.

Because of the fast pace at which the incidents took place, her story is short.

When Kathy and her friends Jill and Shawn reached the top of the hill and took the right turn-off, they all got out of Jill's TransAm to have a look around. Where they could brush aside the long grass and tall goldenrod, they looked for inscriptions on headstones. They were intrigued by the neat inscriptions that began "Here lies . . ." or "In memory of . . ." Not all were readable, however, being too worn by their age and the weather.

Kathy found herself thinking of an epitaph she'd read about in lit. class. Was it Robert Louis Stevenson, the Scottish author? No, I think Shakespeare, she said to herself.

Suddenly Kathy started sneezing and coughing.

"Must be allergic to one of these weeds," she said out loud.

Jill, near Kath at the time, started teasing. "KOF! KOF! KOF! Katherine Olivia Fox!"

"That's silly. Cough isn't spelled KOF, and you know it! Just because J.C. and S.E. don't spell anything in particular, you're jealous. Maybe they would, if I knew your middle initials!"

"Yeah, but it's yours that sounds out to spell cough."

Ignoring Jill, Kathy stopped to set up a marker she had stumbled over. Beside a tangled lilac, this one seemed to have neither names nor dates. Brushing away the mottled late-summer lilac leaves, she turned it over and looked closer. Were those initals? As she bent closer and with her fingertips followed the chiseled-out grooves, she suddenly let out a scream, straightened, and ran for the car. Jill and Shawn, not knowing why, did the same. They piled into Jill's TransAm and headed back to town, leaving the dead to rest in peace.

Safely home and considerably calmed, Kathy told what had upset her. "You'd feel the same, if you'd found a tombstone tipped over on its front, just sort of waiting for you, with no dates on it yet. But there were initials, all right! And they were the exact same as mine: K.O.F."

So far, Kathy has not needed the tombstone.

(45)

UP IN SMOKE

sabel's father told many times about this happening somewhere around Cottonwood in Lyon County.

He was one of eleven children. When it happened, nine were living, along with their parents. Isabel's father was third from the oldest and was thirteen or fourteen at the time the incidents climaxed and ended, so he remembered them clearly.

Every one of the nine children and both parents saw an apparition. Not just all at once, but different ones of the family saw it and at different times. And it continued to appear over the years. It took the shape of a rather smallish woman, always dressed in black. She never talked. She never touched or harmed anyone. But she was always exclusively upstairs.

(47)

She would go in and out of the bedrooms and hall, seeming to be walking but also seeming to go through the walls. At no time did they see her open doors.

This went right on happening and being observed by the family.

When the mysterious woman in black appeared in 1917 or 1918, there had just been a fire. The house burned down to the ground, and the whole family – all nine children and their parents -- stood looking forlornly at the total destruction.

Other people had come to watch the house burn down. Friends and neighbors came and stayed a while, staring at the leaping flames and awkwardly trying to express shock or sympathy. Some offered to help, but there was nothing to do at the time. Finally all had left except the family. They stood huddled closely together, looking at the ashes and embers – all that remained of their home. They stood mesmerized, not yet fully realizing their situation. They stood in shock, immobile, quiescent.

And as they stood and watched, they all saw the same familiar woman figure walk across those hot coals. But this time she was dressed in glorious white and untouched by the fire. They watched her rise and disappear like a poof in the wall of smoke that still lingered over the ruins.

THE GHOSTS OF
LOON LAKE CEMETERY

ome of the old, abandoned cemeteries in the Midwest hold their stories close. Within their fenced areas, hidden under tangled weeds and brush or covered by an accumulation of leathery oak leaves, some tombstones speak of Civil War veterans come home for burial. Others tell of infants who lived for only days or weeks. Still others name several children of the same family, or children and parents, who died within the same year, probably during an epidemic. Some markers are inscribed with loving messages, some with solemn warnings for the living.

There is an abandoned cemetery in Jackson County. The last known burial there was in 1926.

Somehow, ghost and witch stories have become associated with that burial ground, and the legend has increased and changed over the years.

The place is Loon Lake Cemetery, south of Lakefield and not far from Minnesota State

Highway #86, between Petersburg and Sioux Valley. The area boasts a golf course and Loon Lake Grocery Store. The cemetery can be reached either by dry land or by a treacherous, swampy route that newspaper staff writers have been caught in.

This burial place has had its share of visitors, considering that it's abandoned. At first, there were the relatives. They were the family of Horace Alexander Dickinson, who was the father of Lillian Jones of Reading. In October, 1987, Jones told Carrie Sword, a *Worthington Daily Globe* staff writer at the time, that her family used to make it an all-day outing. They would go by horse and buggy up to the cemetery to "tend the graves and the grounds."

There is no longer a road up the pine-covered hill to the graves, but Jones remembers Loon Lake Cemetery as a childhood place. And she remembers that her grandmother is buried there.

It could be that the ghost stories and the legend of a witch's curse began with the same Mary Jane. Mary Jane Dickinson did, according to Jones, have some unusual powers, but she was also a "Christian woman who cared for her ten children and kept her family together," according to Sword's article. Lillian Jones said her grandmother was not a witch, but the legend could have developed because Mary Jane did have ESP.

Other visitors at the cemetery since Jones went there with her family have *not* tended the graves. In fact, there have been frequent beer parties through the years. Perhaps those gatherings spawned the story that as many as three witches are buried there.

The legend rules that anyone who walks there will die an unnatural death. One of the alleged three witches, also named Mary Jane, supposedly died when the people of nearby Petersburg, east of Loon Lake Cemetery, cut off her head with an ax shortly before Halloween in 1881. *That* Mary Jane was *not* the grandmother of Lillian Jones.

Part of the legend of the cemetery is that if one jumps over the graves of one of the witches three times, that person will die. Another detail is that the witches' curse will descend on anyone who misbehaves through rowdiness or vandalism near their graves. Not conducive to a quiet walk alone in the cemetery at dusk.

If the cemetery is haunted, the ghosts could be any of a number of people interred there but still wandering in the vicinity, as spirits, for one reason or another. One of the Mary Janes might be trying to prove her special powers that people ascribe to her. Or the four infants buried there might be looking for their parents, Mr. and Mrs. A. Foshage. Or "J. Pete" isn't happy with the condition of his tombstone, lying in bits in the long grass and weeds, so that visitors can't even pronounce his full name. If he was a pioneer settler, he deserves proper identification. Willie Brown, whose marker bears only his name and the date 1910, could be wanting the rest of his story told. Or Clarinda Allen, who died shortly before Halloween in 1885, might be looking for her relatives.

It is said that when John Dickinson died on October 13, 1877, at the age of 12 years, 9 months, and 22 days, he was the first person buried in Loon Lake Cemetery. That was when Sylvanus Dickinson gave some land to the settlers of Loon Lake. The next spring they moved the bodies of their dead from their homestead burial sites to the cemetery where John Dickinson's body had been buried the previous fall.

That was in the early years, when at least 67 tombstones were upright and a spirit of loving care surrounded them. But now, over 100 years later, the atmosphere is very different. There are the ghost stories, and the legend of the witches' curse lives on. There is the damage done by vandals. According to Jones only 18 stones are still recognizable.

Perhaps one Mary Jane's tombstone is in the bottom of the lake. Perhaps her ghost haunts the

cemetery and the lake, looking for her marker and wanting it rightfully placed. That could, possibly, put an end to the legend and to the apprehension people like young newspaper writers feel about the cemetery.

STEPS TO THE MUSIC

ounds play a part in many ghost stories. Some people hear music from unidentifiable sources. Others hear footsteps.

As a young woman, Orene lived on a farm near Storden in Cottonwood County. She didn't hear music in the walls, but she recalls hearing someone walking up and down the stairs to the second floor. One time when she heard the footsteps, she opened the door at the bottom of the staircase. She could follow the sound on its way up, but she didn't catch the ghost. It seemed to be the case that when members of the family went up or down the stairs to their bedrooms, the other footsteps were never heard. Only when none of the family were using the staircase did they hear the strange sounds.

Orene's younger sister Harriet heard them once and decided to figure it out. She bravely walked up the stairs *behind* the footsteps. Each time she heard a step, she took another careful one up. And she groped courageously ahead with her arms, but she found no one there and felt nothing in the space ahead of her. She was disappointed, and the reason for the sounds remained a mystery.

At about the same time, Orene was interested in learning to play the piano. When she first tried it, she could pick out a melody with her right hand in a sort of pick and peck way, but she couldn't figure out how to chord. Frustrated, she let her attention stray from the keyboard to the sounds of the footsteps on the stairs. The stairway went up from one corner of the same parlor where she sat at the piano. She listened. The footsteps were there again. She was keyed up, and in her nervous state she opened the door and followed the sounds up the steps. Again, she found nothing there. But when she came down, closed the door, and went back to the piano, she found she could play any song she wanted to, even though she couldn't read notes. She was playing by ear.

"Amazing. You should have seen me," she said. "I sat there on the piano stool and lifted my hands and moved my body lightly to the rhythms of the music, like a professional playing for an audience. And I didn't need anyone to turn the page. I just played on and on, from one song to another. It was unbelievable."

Orene was already interested in music. She was frustrated because she couldn't put it all together. Could she, in her keyed-up state at the moment, have developed a special sensitivity that cleared the way for the musical talent to come through? Could a music-loving spirit have somehow moved Orene to a sudden awareness that brought out her potential ability to play the piano almost like a pro?

"NOT IN MY WING!"

ot all college campuses can boast a ghost. For example, SSU at Marshall has none that are known. A letter to the director of residents there brought this reply: "Sorry. Our campus is only 20 years old, so we've not yet had time to develop any lingering spirits."

Lingering spirits. . .a good way to categorize them!

One could deduce, then, that the older campus at Mankato State University *has* had sufficient time

to develop lingering spirits since it was established as Mankato State College in 1866.

By now, the house mothers and the deans of students from the early years as well as the older buildings on Lower Campus are gone. But one couple who lived in an apartment in the first residence hall on Upper Campus recalled a few incidents from their time.

One was the panty raids of the 60's. These raids would start at the large dorms on Lower Campus, about a fourth to a half mile downhill, and the waves of men would come on up the hill to Upper Campus. The male students chanted, "We want pants" and the girls responded by waving their undies out their windows and yelling, "Come get 'em." Once the 400 to 500 boys got into the girls' wing, many drawers were ransacked and emptied of some of their dainty feminine articles of clothing.

In those years, students had no phones in their rooms. The phones were in booths in the halls. When a call came for a student, a buzzer in his or her room would signal from the main desk that there was a call. Then the student, if in the room at the time, took the call out in the corridor.

But during holiday breaks, the buzzers were usually silent. You can imagine the surprise one mid-

night during a vacation, when a buzzer in one of the men's wings sounded. There must have been a two-way connection so that students could also call the main desk.

Two men who because of their work lived more permanently in apartments in Crawford dorm were in. They decided to find out what the call was all about and who was calling. First, they checked the panel for what room needed a connection. When they went to that room, they found that a man had somehow gotten himself locked in. He had used the buzzer to try to get out. When he was finally located, he looked ashen-grey enough to suggest he was a ghost.

Campus ghosts have been known to fit in with the moods of the students, sometimes suggesting that they, themselves, were once students. That makes them happy ghosts or depressed ghosts, depending on how things were going academically or in their love lives. Poor Gertrude, Larsen Hall's ghost on the Luther College Campus in Decorah, Iowa, takes the blame for many mischievous and unexplainable and sometimes downright annoying acts in

Larsen Hall. Some of the campus ghosts, however, are pranksters. That, too, would be typical of student activity.

One spring, on the Mankato campus, a mischievous spirit (no one ever figured out whose) somehow

slipped out of the studying routine and got into a storage room. A ghost wouldn't need a key; it could enter through the wall. This ghost, unassisted, carried armloads of toilet paper rolls out to the parking lot one night, unrolled them deftly in the limited spaces, and stuffed at least 20 cars with the fluffy stuff, to the chagrin of the administrators, faculty, and students the next morning.

Crawford dorm eventually had a fourth wing added. Later, another four-wing complex named McElroy connected with the dining area of Crawford. Crawford-McElroy complex housed 1400 students at one time.

Gage was a new dorm added on the Upper Campus. It was a two-wing high rise with 12 stories. What a lot of campus life the many high windows in Gage must have looked down on! What a lot of incidents the dorm walls could tell if walls could record and spill those tales!

So there you have it. It seems there are several possiblities if anyone is looking for a campus ghost at Mankato State University. One is the ghost of a man locked in a room during the holidays, still trying the buzzers for help to get out.

Another likely one is the spirit of a male student from the panty raids, still wandering the halls or the campus green, looking for souvenirs.

Then there's the possibility that the student with a flair for interior decorating might be hanging around, in spirit, to see if he can get by with it again.

Or maybe the large-bodied housemother who tried to hold off the wave of panty-raiders by going down the hall in her bathrobe and curlers, swinging a pop bottle and shouting, "They'll never get into my wing!" is, in spirit, still guarding her "Corregidors."

In fact, since MSU has grown so rapidly (it proudly claims to have nearly 15,000 students with the Crawford-McElroy Complex and the Gage high-rises housing only about 3,000 of them), there could very well be several more lingering spirits to watch out for on those late nights out under the full moon!

DEATH RAPS RECOGNIZED

orraine's first experience with a ghost in her family happened when she was only four, when her mother's parents were living with them.

Grandmother was very sick in the hospital in near-by Sioux City on that particular day. Lorraine was at the foot of the stairs in their home in Southwest Minnesota when something or someone came sliding down the banister. Lorraine told her mother about it. Her mother looked up and said, "Lorraine, there's no one there. But Grandma's very sick. Maybe it's Grandma -- or the spirit of Grandma."

From that moment on, Lorraine's mother stayed close to her daughter as though she knew strange things would happen and she didn't want her child to be frightened by them.

That night, a wind-up alarm clock fell off the dresser and onto the floor. It landed face down. It stopped at four a.m. -- the exact time that the grandmother died. Lorraine remembers hearing

the family talking about that. Was it a coincidence, or was it a signal?

After that grandmother's death, the family moved to another house. Grandpa stayed with them, and he lived upstairs. He hardly ever got out of bed due to the weakness of old age.

About a year later, another clock fell off the dresser. It was a beautiful porcelain boudoir clock, and it had always been kept beside Lorraine's mother's bed. It landed face down that night, and it stopped at the time of Grandpa's death.

To the family, this seemed more than just a coincidence.

A few years later, when Lorraine was nine, her grandmother on her father's side was in the hospital in Sioux City. That December, the doctors diagnosed her illness as cancer.

At that time, Lorraine's father always left for work by 5:30 a.m. Lorraine's mother got up to get breakfast for him. One morning, after he left, she had gone back upstairs to bed as she usually did. About an hour later, the piano downstairs started playing. It woke the whole family. Lorraine's mother said, "The cat is probably walking on the keys."

Lorraine went downstairs to check. The cat wasn't

anywhere to be seen. In fact, the piano keyboard was closed.

Lorraine and her mother went back to bed, but the mother had recognized the incident as another death rap.

These signals had been following Lorraine's mother all her life. This time, she got in bed with the children so as to be near them until it was time for them to get up for school. About nine o'clock that morning, while the children were in school, the call came at the house. Grandmother (Lorraine's father's mother) had passed away.

When Lorraine was almost twelve and after another move to another house in Southwest Minnesota, something else occurred. Aunt Zephrey, Lorraine's mother's aunt, was married to a peace officer in another state. The officer was transporting a prisoner to a facility in a larger city. Somehow the prisoner jumped the sheriff and killed him. A clock stopped again. It was another

windup. It fell off the stand beside Lorraine's mother's bed in the daytime. Later that day, the call came relaying the message that the sheriff had died.

Lorraine said there were eight children in her mother's family: her mother, six aunts, and one uncle to Lorraine. All but three had died before Lorraine's own mother died at age 59. Each time one died, there was a signal she called a death rap, so she would know.

When Lorraine's Dad's mother died, the piano had played. When her Dad's father died, the signal was different. He died after attending a wrestling match. He got in the car to go home and had a heart attack. At the time, those at home were playing cards. Lorraine's mother looked at her husband and said, "There's something wrong." Then, for no apparent reason, the pot of coffee she had gotten up to make fell from her hand. Fifteen minutes later the call came informing the family that Grandpa had died of the heart attack.

Lorraine's parents had been living in their own home when Lorraine's mother died in 1974. After the funeral, Lorraine's Dad couldn't go into the bedroom his wife had used for hers. Each time he approached the door, he heard the music of heavenly choirs.

During the night that Lorraine's mother died in the hospital at about six p.m., Lorraine's mother also appeared at the house and talked kindly and gently to her daughter. She asked her daughter not to argue about dividing the belongings, and to let Father live with her and her husband. And he did just that. But Lorraine's mother was in the hospital in Sioux City and she had died at six p.m. Yet she appeared later that same night, in the house where her parents lived up until the time of that death.

About a year and a half ago, Lorraine's father died. He had lived with Lorraine and her husband in Worthington, according to the last wish of his wife. He never felt quite at ease there, though. And it was through no fault of his daughter's, nor his son-in-law's. He just never wanted the door to his room closed. He wanted to hear their voices and be near the people he loved.

After his death, Lorraine herself wanted the door closed. It was an extra bedroom and now that they no longer needed to keep it warm, they could shut the register and the door and save on the heating costs. But the door wouldn't stay shut, even when it was closed all the way and the latch caught. The thought came to Lorraine then that her father's spirit didn't want to be away from his family.

What a close family! And what a good spirit among them -- each time of a death, a gentle announcement or a signal to let them know. After the deaths occurred, signs that the departed still dwelt among them. In spirit.

(71)

A SCRAP OF CLOTH

ee's mother was born in 1889, just a century ago now. She and her three sisters told their children later on that on the farmplace where they lived as girls, something wasn't right.

The farm was in one of the counties near the southern border of Minnesota. There was a cemetery next to the farm. This was back in the horse and buggy days, when horses were needed for transportation and field work.

But when the horses on that farm were in the barn, they could often be heard stomping and snorting as though fighting something off or fighting amongst themselves. After the girls once heard those sounds, they didn't go very close to the barn, but their father did. He would hear the sounds of boards being ripped loose and flying around, hitting the walls and other things inside the barn. He

(73)

expected more than once to spend time and energy clearing the debris off the feed bunks and  the floor. He thought surely all the hay racks would have to be straightened and the feed boxes put up again. But when he went in to check, he found the horses quiet, no boards loose, everything in order.

On another occasion on the same place, the girls' father, the farmer, came up from the barn on a winter day. As he approached the house, he saw that his wife was hanging the washing on the lines. The shirts and overalls were quickly freezing to the line  and swaying stiffly in the bitter cold air.

He asked her if supper was ready. She didn't answer, so he figured she was cold and just wanted to finish up fast. He went on into the house, where he found his wife in the kitchen, stirring a pot of steaming stew.

They both looked around outside. They found no one out there, no clothes basket, and no clothes on the line. Just a fragment of grey cloth frozen to the line under one clothespin. That made such an impression on the girls that they never forgot it.

In the same house, Dee and her sisters often heard someone walking around upstairs. When they went up to look, there was no one. All was in order.

Later, the parents sold the house to another family who were openly told it was haunted. The new owners also heard the horses stomping in the barn and heard footsteps upstairs in the house. They asked their priest to come over and see what he could do.

The priest came. His decisive action took place *outside* the house and barn. He walked around in the cemetery next to the fenceline. He did whatever a priest does in such a situation and with such a request for help. After he left, the new owners heard no more unexplainable noises.

The original buildings on the farm are all gone now, but the cemetery is still there, just over the half-buried fence.

SAVED BY THE BELL

hy not? It's Halloween, but what can happen? Do you think there's someone in that old building?

"Naw. It hasn't been used for years. C'mon! Let's go."

"O.K. But we all stick together, whatever happens. Agreed?"

"Like glue. Even if it's scary, I'll take a challenge any day!"

"Or night?"

"Or night. You bet!" And with Jamie's last remark, the three friends headed for the old schoolhouse.

It was almost midnight, but their parents wouldn't be missing them. All three kids worked at the A&W at the edge of town and had just gotten off work. Jamie and Tom felt safe when they walked by their house, on the way toward the center of town. All the lights were off except the porch light. That meant their mom and dad were off in dreamland. Rich lived just beyond the school. He wouldn't be going by his house until after their adventure.

The old brick schoolhouse was just one of the dilapidated buildings in this ghost town, one of several in Southwest Minnesota. It hadn't been

used as a school since consolidation. It was considered too run down to repair. No one even believed it could be restored, though there was some talk about that later on. It was simply a relic of the years when it stood as a symbol in the once-booming town. Now owls spooked the place at night with

their Who-who-hoo-hoo-hoo and their Who-who-what-what-what. And bats flew in and out of the bell tower at regular hours.

The three adventurers went around to the janitor's door at the back. They found the door swaying on one hinge. Inside, they were pitched into complete darkness. Rich took out his pocket flashlight. Cardboard barrels either upright or rolling on their sides confronted them, making it hard to get through to the long hall.

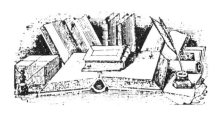

Once they reached the hall, they were able to find a first-floor classroom. There they found everything in complete disorder, except for the teacher's desk.

It was as neat and organized as if someone were ready for the next day of school. The few remaining students' desks were either turned over and broken or, if standing whole, were cleared of their papers and pencils.

On a shelf at the side of one room, stacks of books waited to be passed out. On the board were lists of names, each with a set of figures. Were they demerit marks? It was hard to read the chalk writing, with Rich's flashlight flickering dimmer every minute.

The three decided to move on to the gym. They found it and went in cautiously. The doors slammed behind them.

"No! Now we're in complete dark!"

"What's the matter with your flashlight?"

"Why didn't *you* bring one?"

They were all shouting at once. They tried to open the doors, but they seemed to have locked automatically when they slammed.

"There has to be an exit. You have to be able to get out of a gym," Tom said, a little too loudly it seemed to the others. He and Jamie started down one wall, feeling their way to the corner and the adjacent wall while Rich did the same, going the other direction.

Before long Tom's voice broke into the night.

"Here! I found it! Here's the other door. I knew there had to be one near the bleachers!"

They all pushed on the door until it creaked open far enough for them to get out to the hall again. Then they took the short stairway down to the boiler room.

Down there, a little light came in through the dirty window. "Must be from the street light at the back alley," Rich mused.

"Good!" Jamie said. "I'll take every bit of light I can get. It's too spooky in here!"

"Hey, Jamie, girl or not, don't go chicken on us. We're all in this together and we stick together to the end. Remember?"

"All right. But it's still spooky. What now?" And they moved toward a door that hung open and found themselves out in a hall.

Suddenly they heard noises. It sounded like a door opened and closed down the hall. Then they heard muted voices, as of a teacher giving instructions in low tones. As of children reciting and singing. As of their own hearts pounding.

Their breathing came fast and shallow as they tried to stay quiet. Jamie whispered, "That sounds like someone cranking a pencil sharpener."

Tom thought he heard chalk screeching on a blackboard as he stood frozen on the spot. When the sounds quieted down, the three found their way back to the classroom they had visited earlier. But now the desks were all upright. The books from the shelf were open on the desks.

"It must be an English classroom," Rich told the others. "Look at that big poster. It says, 'An example of a simile: I just washed my hair. It looks like Angel Flake coconut, all white and curly.' "

The light was on now, so they could see all of this. That was the most surprising. And on the board, under TODAY IS OCTOBER 31, 1981, the lists of names and figures were changed. The only writing on the wall now was: JAMIE TOWNE . . . RICHARD SPENCER . . . THOMAS TOWNE.

"What the--? Who else knows we're in here?"

"Did you tell anyone where we were going?"

"How could I? We didn't decide until we were blocks from the A&W! Who could have been in here since we were, before?"

Then, in the dead of night, the school bell began to ring up in the roof tower. Not like for a school day. It was more like the slow knell of a tolling bell. And it tolled on and  on and on. It was creepy enough already, but Jamie started counting and kept on until it quit. It rang out enough times to total their ages! Fifty one!

"Wow! That's enough noise to wake the dead!"

"Or our parents--or the sheriff or any one else that's asleep."

"But how did it ring? Someone had to pull the rope in the main entry!"

They started moving cautiously in case someone else was in the building and intended to do them harm.

In the lights from the cars pulling into the circular driveway, the kids saw Pat, a former custodian, up in the stairway balcony rhythmically pulling on the bell rope. Everyone knew he had been dead for forty-some years. What the people of the ghost town didn't know was that he still came back at night, without pay, to look after his building and protect it from vandals. He hated the mess they made. He always straightened up again at night, swept the floors, and had things ready for the teachers when they came the next morning.

"He must even write their lessons and lists on the board for them," Jamie whispered.

Tom added, "And now that he's done his work once more, he can ring the bell and announce a new day."

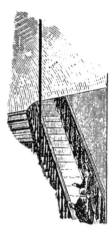

They huddled in the front entry and watched. But moments later, when their anxious parents met their teenagers at the front doors, there was no custodian to be seen. Just Rich and Tom and Jamie and their parents, who heard the bell ringing, checked their clocks, and found that their teenagers weren't home yet from work. And the sheriff and a few others showed up, awakened by the bell that had for so many years also called them to school.

From that Halloween night on, the hundred or so citizens of the ghost town seemed to respect the abandoned schoolhouse more than before. And Jamie, Tom, and Rich never walked by it again after work.

HEAVENLY CHOIRS

ora lives in an old white frame house that has been improved sometime in the past. Her parents had lived there for a few years before she moved in with them. Then, as her parents grew older, she looked after them.

It all started the day after Dora's father died. Things started moving. She never knew what would move next, or where. First it was a plate on the kitchen counter. Then a glass on the table. Then an ash tray slid across the coffee table top.

Dora really had plenty to do to complete the funeral arrangements, clean the house for company, and be ready for callers. Yet within those few days before the funeral, objects kept moving before her troubled eyes. When she started checking for logical reasons, she found no moisture under the glass, no slant to the counter, no reason for the ash tray to scoot across the coffee table top. She decided this was one of those situations that called for an emphatic confrontation. She said, loudly, "Go away! Leave me alone! I have work to do. I don't need this, too!"

Whatever it was, it left. And the funeral was conducted peacefully, with no upsetting incidents.

Some time later, Dora's mother died. A week after the funeral, Dora sat in the den reading the paper, with Poco on her lap. Poco wasn't very big. That's why he was named Poco, making use of a musical term for a little bit of anything, like a little more lively, a little bit slower, or anything else in small amounts. Poco, small to begin with, did grow -- but only a little, by small degrees, gradually.

While Dora read her mother's obituary, Poco suddenly got up and jumped down off her lap. He looked toward the living room and wagged his tail as if he recognized someone who had just come in. He joyfully welcomed the visitor. Dora was dumbfounded. No one had knocked. She'd heard no one come in, and she saw no one by the door. But Poco went into the front room and very carefully walked around a spot as if someone was standing there. Then he pawed at the invisible guest's ankles, begging for attention. Dora saw no ghost, but one must have been there because Poco acted exactly as he always had when Dora's mother returned from her walk.

But the strangest incident Dora related was somehow connected with a photo- graph and the people in it.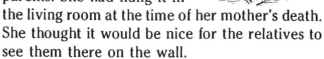

Dora has a large, framed black and white photo of her parents. She had hung it in the living room at the time of her mother's death. She thought it would be nice for the relatives to see them there on the wall.

After the funeral, Dora heard music in the evening. Yet she had nothing playing. At first, she thought maybe the neighbors had their stereo on. Or maybe there were some teenagers in the neighborhood with their car radio turned up. The music got louder and louder. Dora went out on the porch, only to find there were no cars. She heard no music coming from the other houses in the block. She went back in to see if her radio was on, but it wasn't. She even unplugged the TV. The music got even louder. Then it stopped.

This thing with the music happened several times over a month or more. Once, Dora called her sister in another county to let her listen to the loud music over the phone. Elizabeth couldn't hear it. Dora tried to tape it, but the elusive strains managed to not be recorded. The more Dora heard the music, though, the more familiar it became. She couldn't recognize the compositions by name, but it dawned on her that she was hearing beautiful organ music with its moving crescendos, like that she had heard when she played recordings of the Mormon Tabernacle Choir or a similar group.

(87)

After a couple months, Dora decided to rearrange the furniture in the living room. She hung her parents' photo in another room. The music was suddenly absent.

After a while, Dora had the thought to put the photo back where she'd had it at the time of her mother's funeral. She wanted to see what would happen. She tried it, and she heard the music again. The moving strains were nice to hear – but disturbing, too. Where did they come from?

A natural question directed to Dora after listening to her story was, "Did music play a significant part in your life earlier or in the lives of your parents?"

And she slowly answered, "Well . . . yes . . . but I'd never though about that. I did sing solos for a time, mostly patriotic songs for conventions and other group meetings. And . . . before that . . . I sang at the top of my lungs, walking to school and back. I guess I started singing when I was five. And Mother whistled and Dad sang as they went about their work on the farm. My sis and I always knew just where they were. We felt a closeness in the family when we heard their music.

"Yes, now that you have me thinking about it, music *was* a noticeable part of our lives. Not just mine, but the whole family's. Now, I wonder what the connection could have been between the photo and the music. Do you suppose my father, who loved to sing and who died first, didn't want to leave his wife and daughters, so he hung around and let us know he was there by the sweet strains of heavenly choirs?"

A SWINGING RED LANTERN

armers reported seeing a man swinging a glowing red lantern and walking on the Omaha Railroad tracks south of Le Sueur. Neighbors said someone lived in a cave in the hollow along the road to Ottawa. Young couples out for a moonlight stroll didn't loiter long.

It was generally thought that the man with the lantern haunted the area. But no one wanting to communicate with him could approach him successfully. When they tried, he disappeared. Whoever it was, he became known as the Le Sueur Brewery ghost.

The area was Old Brewery Hill. John remembered his father and other old-timers talking about the "spirit," and John kept the story in mind for many years. He said it went way back to when the brewery burned down.

According to Tom Conroy's account in the *Le Sueur News-Herald* of November 18, 1986, a man named George Kienzli started the brewery in about 1875. Kienzli put up a small building and dug two cellars into the hills. He used large wooden casks in one of these to age the beer. He packed ice into the other one to cool the beer in warm weather.

Several men worked for Kienzli. They brewed the beer each week and they hauled it to Arlington, Henderson, and Le Sueur. Near the brewery, cattle were fattened on the by-products.

Two others after Kienzli bought the business, but neither operated it long. Then it was closed. But just east of the Ottawa road, the remains of the cellars can still be seen by those who know which side of which hill to examine.

The building itself burned down, but the stories grew about the ghost that haunted the area. They were retold by Ruth Kinsey in the *Le Sueur News Herald* of October 26, 1960, reprinted from a 1936

New Ulm newspaper. It was believed that a man lived in one of the caves. People said they saw him come from the cave and, carrying his red lantern, walk on the tracks. But he and his lantern seemed to dissolve whenever anyone tried to catch him.

One of the stories was that he paid no attention to trains on the track, nor to their warning whistles. He just kept on walking along, swinging the lantern. One train stopped to get his attention. When the brakeman stepped down to get the man off the tracks, there was no one there. That happened more than once.

People were concerned. Someone checked the caves and found some old clothes, a straw tick, a shoe box, and some bones.

Yet someone was seen going in and out of the cave at night.

For a while, no one wanted to live in the house across from the old brewery site. Later, someone  built a new house there, and they said the hollow was peaceful in their time. But people who remember the early stories, even those about hearing noises like machinery running in the cave, walk by quickly. They wonder if they can pass the hill without seeing the man and his swinging red lantern moving on down the tracks or finding his way back to his cave in the side of Old Brewery Hill.

SOME GHOSTS BRING PEACE

hat would you do if, when you considered buying a house, neighbors told you it was haunted? Well, it didn't worry Edna and Herman. They bought it anyway, thirty-five years ago, and moved in.

Then the happenings started. Little things, at first. Like one night when all the family were in their rooms, ready for a night's sleep. Some were in second floor bedrooms. The youngest was in the first floor bedroom. And one was on the davenport. That one saw a shape going down the hall. Edna and Herman heard a noise as if someone had walked out the door. All the family heard it, wherever they were. The parents checked but found no one missing.

When Edna's mother died, a neighbor "sat the house" the day of the funeral. As the volunteer sat dozing in the rocking chair, she suddenly woke up to find Edna's mother in the room. She was wearing a blue flowered dress and a gold brooch -- the same dress and brooch she had been dressed in before they laid her in her casket.

(95)

The ghost spoke to the surprised house-sitter. She said, "I wanted to see how much remodeling Herman had got done – wanted to see how it was coming along, before I leave. But I'd better go now, or I'll be late for my own funeral." This happened about two hours before the service, while the family was out having dinner.

After Edna's husband Herman died, his widow and their youngest daughter could hear music coming from a corner of the living room, no matter where they sat. Several times, one of them got up to make sure the radio and TV were off. They were. The music was all Irish and Scottish, played softly until late hours, as if the absent loved one wanted them to relax, now that it was over. Friends and neighbors who stopped in heard the music, too, and it was very relaxing for all. Sometimes the family and guests also heard voices coming from above the ceiling, near a fireplace in one corner of the living room.

Some time later, Edna remarried. The couple occupied the same house she and Herman had first bought. One night when the two were playing cards at the kitchen table, they both saw Herman come from a back room into the front of the house and go out the front door. It had to be Herman's ghost, Edna thought. Who else? But what a strange situation.

Another time, at dusk, Edna and her second husband were playing cards when Edna excused herself to go to the bathroom. On her way back, she saw something or someone floating up and around over the plants in the living room against the window. Then the shape disappeared. It seem-ed to rise toward the ceiling and was gone. Edna sensed a calmness in herself. She wondered if she had just seen the spirit of her mother. When Edna went back to the card game, her partner took  one look at her and said, "You saw something! Was it another ghost? I can tell by the look on your face."

Then Edna told him about the time a month or  so earlier when she couldn't sleep. She had sat on the loveseat in the living room with a cup of warm milk, try-ing to lure sleep. It was close to midnight when she saw something moving outside the window. It was a shape hovering above the flowers. She moved closer to look out. The shape spoke. Through the window, Edna heard, "I'm an angel. I came down here with your mother. She wants to see your flowers. She always loved them so, but don't let her see you. She doesn't want to frighten you."

Edna backed up from the window and watched from there. She saw one shape moving out by the road and another by the flowerbed. "Then they both moved away," she said, "leaving me feeling very peaceful."

"After that," Edna continued, "we got out the Ouija Board. We asked it, 'Was that a ghost?' It went to NO. 'What was it, then?' It spelled out the word SPIRIT. We hadn't thought of that. 'My mother's?' I asked. And the board went right to YES."

A son-in-law of Edna's died of cancer at age thirty-nine, just a few years before this story was told. One night Edna and her husband were sitting in the living room. Suddenly the room turned cold. They couldn't figure it out. After all, it was July! They reached for the afghans and were more comfortable. One of them checked the other rooms, and they were all as warm as one would expect.

After they went to bed that night, Edna started thinking about it again. She got up and went out to the living room. She sat down on the love seat in the dark room. It was still cold there. Was it a cold spot? Was there a message for her?

Edna asked, "What?"

Then a strong scent of roses in bloom pervaded the room while a voice like that of her son-in-law said, "There's going to be an accident."

Edna didn't want to hear that message. She went to bed and covered her ears. But that didn't end it. She was frightened now. She kept thinking about the cold room and the roses and the message.

It was still July. Six or seven friends sat around the kitchen table playing cards. Edna felt the cold and smelled the roses. Then she heard the same voice as before, with the same message: "Be careful, Mother. There's going to be an accident. It could be you."

In the next little while, Edna left for work. She had been working a night shift. "On the way," she said, "I tried to stay calm and be careful. But I looked up to see a semi in my path. A car was trying to pass the semi and coming right at me. I knew we would crash head-on. The feeling of cold and the fragrance of roses filled the car." The next second, she found herself stopped on the shoulder, just as the oncoming car went by. She was O.K. "The ghost," she explained, "had protected me. Saved me."

Edna and her husband and a grandson who spends a lot of time at their house have been puzzled about the strange noises they hear, like little crashes. Edna finally called a pastor and told him about the things that had been happening. He told Edna, "Someone died in or near the house several years ago. I know that, but I don't know *how* he died." Edna wonders if some of the sounds and forms are the spirit of the person who died -- not wanting to leave, not ready to make the break, or having some unfinished business to take care of.

Currently, the couple and their grandson still hear footsteps going upstairs and crossing the hall into the big room, where the bed is always made up. Several times they have found the covers pulled back on that bed and the pillow dented as if someone had slept there. This was 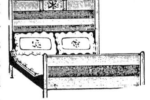 so upsetting that Edna, who had usually felt calm and at peace with the ghosts of the house, actually called the police to check the bed before the covers were once more pulled up over the pillow.

Neither these strange occurrences nor the actions of the huge tree behind the house have sent the family away. "That tree," Edna told me, "has a life of its own. Like a cat with nine lives. At one time that old tree had four large trunks, like four trees in one. In 1972 one trunk fell on our two cars. In 1974, one trunk fell across the dining room and caved in the roof during a storm. In August of 1976, a tornado hit Heron Lake. Every light in town went out. The largest trunk of the tree, the only one remaining, crashed against the back of our house, causing extensive damage. It was almost as if the tree was holding our house so the tornado couldn't blow it away. Like giant arms, the branches still on that trunk reached across to each side and over the top of the house, securing it, though damaging it, too."

Perhaps the tree has not only been a tree. Perhaps its four trunks, now diminished to one huge, tall, roughly shaped stub of a trunk, figured more in the history of the house and its spirits than anyone will ever know.

NOT READY TO GO

hen Percy was in the hospital, his grandfather had been dead for several years. Nevertheless, he appeared to Percy's wife Pauline and announced, "I'm ready to take Percy back with me."

Being a spirited woman, Pauline spoke up. She said, "No, you don't! He's not ready to go yet!"

Later on, when Percy died, there were all the usual details to take care of. His widow Pauline and son Doug visited with the other mourners and accepted their condolences during the serving of the lunch. Pauline told the ladies in charge where the floral arrangements and potted plants should be given. Finally they could go home.

While Pauline followed Doug across the porch, she was thinking that the house would be quiet, and right now it would be a relief.

Once inside, she put her purse and gloves down on the little table in the hall. Then she started toward the living room. That was when she screamed.

From the next room, Doug asked, "What's wrong?"

Pauline gathered all her courage to answer him. Even then, her voice trembled. "Well . . . looks like . . . your father . . . beat us home. He's . . . . standing in the front room."

Doug had a hard time believing that, so he looked, and he saw his father there, too.

Percy kept coming back now and then. He had one stiff leg, so when he was there, the family could easily recognize him by the sounds he made going up and down the stairs. He would skip every other step. That made the stairs easier.

Once upstairs, Percy would enter the bedroom where he'd slept before he took sick. There he just sat and rocked, and he came and went as he pleased.

One day Doug brought an antenna downstairs. He planned to put it on the car. It was one of those ten to twelve foot whips, and Doug's mother cautioned him, "Be careful, son. Don't mark the ceiling with that."

In the next moment, it must have been Percy's ghost that bent the flexible top of the antenna down so it wouldn't do any harm.

After a while, Pauline gave her son the hutch that Percy had used to display his collection of miniature farm animals. He had always kept these figures on the shelves in a certain pattern, without variation. That way, he knew just where each one should be and he could tell immediately if any were missing.

It soon became Doug's wife's duty to dust the hutch. When she did, Dorothy rearranged the animals three times to suit her own tastes. She hardly thought it would hurt to move them around a little since she had to move them anyway to dust.

But each time, Percy's ghost came during the night and put them back just as he had left them. As he did this, Dorothy could hear the sounds of the animals being moved. She found it hard to sleep soundly once she figured out what was happening.

Finally Doug told his wife, "You'll learn to leave Dad's animals alone."

(105)

And now she does. When she dusts, she puts each animal back just where Percy apparently wanted it.

After a time, Doug's mother married again. Her second husband's name was Ray. In their home, in the kitchen, Ray sometimes felt an extraordinary chill. He believed it was the signal that Pauline's mother, as a spirit, would come to visit. Moments later, the family could recognize the fragrance of her favorite perfume.

 One day Ray drove his pickup to a distant place, but it seemed he was not alone. The scent of Pauline's mother's perfume accompanied him in the pickup for the whole day's ride.

Ray said, "I didn't think it was any more strange than this story about a house near the A&W root beer stand in Worthington. They say a woman died in the house. Then the man who owned it rented it to a young couple. Sometimes they left their dishes in the sink and moved on to things they'd rather be doing.

"During the night, and first thing in the morning when they woke up, they'd hear a lot of clattering in the kitchen. When they went out there for breakfast, they'd find the dishes done and in their places in the cupboards.

"I think," Ray concluded, "there must be some spirits that take pleasure in making life more pleasant for the living."

ANNIE MARY'S RESTLESS SPIRIT

n Albin Township in the southern part of Brown County, the story of Annie Mary's restless spirit is known by many.

Annie Mary died when she was six. Her grave is on what was her parents' farm, the old Twente place, about 18 miles southwest of New Ulm. It's just west of Hanska and a little farther northwest from Madelia. Robert and Karen Fischer are the current owners and occupants of the farm.

There has been some disagreement as to the cause of Annie Mary's death. Some say she fell from a hayloft soon after her sixth birthday, was injured, and didn't recover. Some say she had scarlet fever and slipped into a coma, causing her parents, Richard and Lizzie Twente, to believe she was dead.

However, the Brown County Death Records indicate that Annie Mary Twente, the second of five girls, died of a natural cause -- "lung fever" -- on October 25, 1886, at age six. Lizzie Twente's foster granddaughter, now living at Willmar, was told by her mother that Annie Mary died of diphtheria.

In 1886, the death of a child was not terribly unusual, whatever the cause. Neither was the location of Annie Mary's burial site. Many early settlers buried their dead on their own land.

 But the duration of her first interment was unusual, if one believes the stories.

One part of the legend is that Annie Mary's mother, Lizzie (Elizabeth), felt that they might have buried their daughter alive. When the grave was opened, the inside of the coffin supposedly showed signs of a struggle. There were scratches. Annie Mary's face, which should have been fixed in repose, was instead fixed in terror and her eyes were wide open. She had reportedly torn out a clump of her hair in her deep despair. According to the tales, the body was definitely not in the same condition it was in when it was placed in the coffin.

Numerous news staff writers have retold the story,

OCTOBER

at least twice in Halloween issues in 1979 and 1980 and once in June, 1986. But then, Annie Mary's birth and death both occurred in October, 1880 and 1886. Articles were printed on the hundredth anniversary of her birth and death. Readers recall seeing the story in the *Mankato Free Press*, the *New Ulm Journal*, the *St. James Plaindealer*, and other papers. The legend's details were provided by news writers, the Fischers, and their neighbors. The Brown County Historical Society filled in some of the facts.

One of the articles gives credit to the late Art Guttum for information about Annie Mary Twente's first burial site. Though Guttum died early in 1989, he had farmed near the old Twente place. He told a staff writer that the little girl was first interred in the Iberia Cemetery, but her father didn't approve. Perhaps his reason was that it was in Stark Township, too far north. Or perhaps he could already tell that the cemetery was fast becoming an abandoned one.

So Richard Twente chose a place in the corner of his 160 acres which he had purchased in August of 1884 for $1,140. He moved Annie Mary's coffin to the chosen spot, on the highest point of his land and overlooking the farm. In 1914, the farm was sold to the grandfather of Robert Fischer, present owner, and the little Twente girl is still buried there.

It could be that the legend speaks of the grave being opened because Richard Twente moved its contents from the cemetery to his own land.

Guttum said that after Richard Twente buried his daughter for the second time, he put up a wooden fence around her grave. That didn't satisfy him, so he had a plasterer help him build an 18-inch thick, four-foot high wall of stone and mortar.  They installed an iron gate with a brass lock. Neighbors remembered seeing the gate and lock as they drove by on the old wagon trail between Albin Township and its neighbor to the east, Lake Hanska Township.

The key to the gate's lock was found many years later, among the possessions of one of Annie Mary's sisters. That sister was Elizabeth, born four years after Annie Mary. Elizabeth's foster daughter, also named Elizabeth (Thissen), still has the key. But it seems the gate and the enclosure could not contain the spirit of the young girl buried there.

The story is that when the gate is open, her restless spirit dressed in white wanders on the hillside in the moonlight.

They say that car headlights suddenly fail as people drive by the enclosure. Two young boys who visited the site one night reportedly had a frightening experience. One climbed the tree near the wall, lost consciousness and fell, and had to be taken to a hospital. It is said that doctors could not explain what was wrong with him.

Other tales are told, such as that on hot days, the stone is cold and vice versa. Others tell that cars

stall on the bridge nearby, horses refuse to cross it or are spooked there, and the ground just in front of the marker is barren. But there used to be a peony bush that bloomed every spring for Annie Mary and her family.

The tombstone of gray granite has been broken from its base. As the saplings grew, their roots pushed up under the marker and tilted it. The black iron gate is gone, but the hinges are still in the wall. The enclosure is overgrown with weeds and grass and brush, and it's often littered with empty cans and paper trash. The wall itself is cracked, and moss has begun to form a mosaic on it.

Perhaps Richard Twente once thought the plot would also become the burial place for him and his wife. There was enough space. A tree was planted on each side of the entrance; one, an ash, still stands.

The other is merely a charred stump. Though there are signs of wear, the inscription on the stone can still be read. It says, "ANNIE MARY / Born / Oct. 14, 1880 / Died / Oct. 26, 1886 / Father and Mother, May I meet you in your royal court on high. / TWENTE."

Stories about Richard Twente's unusual personality have perhaps added to the legend. When he brought his family to Brown County from Kentucky, his religion was different from that of his neighbors. That may have caused them to see him as very strange. But they soon found that he was also brilliant and enterprising. He sold nursery stock. In 1918 he wrote and copyrighted a pamphlet about planting fruits and fruit trees.

He was very strong physically. He built a large,  three-level barn with a stone foundation, with only the help of his wife and girls. For a long time, it was the biggest barn in the area. In the mid-1880's, he built a granary that was for many years listed on the National Register of Historic Places. It had a scale for weighing, a hoist and belt system, and seven bins on the upper levels. And Twente put up a two-level hoghouse, also with help of his wife and living daughters.

But Richard Twente also did some strange things, according to the people who know the legend. Once he started across the prairie in a sled,  taking his wife and daughters with him. The only reason he turned back was that his wife begged

him to, so they wouldn't all freeze to death. Some say people were afraid of him because of his fits of anger and his extreme strength.

Once, he left his family and went to Canada where he bought some "worthless land." Before long, he contacted his wife and tried to borrow $10 from her "to buy bread so I won't starve."

(113)

Robert Fischer, who grew up on the old Twente farm, says that Richard Twente dug up Annie Mary's body twice. Once, it was because he thought the corpse might have been stolen.

Richard Twente died around 1920 while in Canada

cutting or hauling wood. His riderless horse went to a neighbor's place. When the neighbors investigated, they found Richard Twente had died of a heart attack. He is buried next to his wife Lizzie and some of her sisters in the Methodist Cemetery at Raymond. Lizzie had gone to live near there with her daughter Elizabeth for a time. Elizabeth's foster daughter said that Lizzie died in 1936.

Apparently it was someone else who tried to dig into the grave as recently as 1985. Robert Fischer shoveled the dirt back to fill the hole again.

Some who have studied the phenomenon of spirits of the ghostly kind say that ghosts are the dead who are stuck on earth. A spirit may be waiting for something, such as a decent, secure burial.

Annie Mary had a decent burial at least twice. But when her white-clad spirit roams the hillside on moonlit nights, she has reason to be displeased. Her iron gate is gone, her wall is cracked, thistles

(114)

form a tangle in the enclosure, and her tombstone is no longer intact.

A pastor of the Lake Hanska and LaSalle Lutheran Churches once asked Fischer to think about having the grave moved, once more, in an attempt to avoid the disrespect and vandalism at the site. Perhaps, if that were done . . . or if the wall and tombstone were repaired . . . or if the gate were located and once again hung on its hinges and closed . . . and the key were turned in the brass lock one final turn . . . perhaps, then, the restless spirit of Annie Mary Twente could rest peacefully. It is time.

NOT JUST A DREAM

 ometimes a hand resting on one's shoulder is comforting. Sometimes it's . . . surprising.

First, let me introduce Aunt Minnie.

Mrs. Alex Walker of Magnolia in Rock County was Aunt Minnie to her family. Since she was a sister to Georgette (Mrs. G.O. Bigelow) who lived in St. James, she was Aunt Minnie to Georgette's daughter Lois (now Mrs. Clayton R. Johnson of Worthington).

About 25 years ago, the Johnsons were visiting friends in Rochester in Southeast Minnesota. One morning at the breakfast table, Lois recalled a dream she'd had the night before. Though it's hard for her to remember the details so  much later, she does remember that her Aunt Minnie appeared. She was sitting in a chair in the same room with Lois.

(117)

"I put my hand on her shoulder for a few seconds," Lois told those around her, "and I asked her, 'How are you, Aunt Minnie?' It seemed so natural, because I knew she hadn't been well.

"Aunt Minnie's answer surprised me. She said, 'I've come home to die.' "

The others around the table were surprised, too. Mrs. Walker had been in a care center at Mountain Lake, between St. James and Worthington. Though she hadn't been well and had been there for a while, death was not expected at the time.

After Lois told her dream, she said, "After all, it was only a dream. Nothing like this has ever happened to me before. Let's not let it shake us up. We must have been talking about Aunt Minnie last night before we went to bed."

Later that morning, the Johnsons left the home of their Rochester friends to return to their own home in Worthington. On the way, they stopped in St. James to see Lois' parents, the Bigelows. The first thing Mrs. Bigelow said when Lois and Clayton greeted her parents was, "Aunt Minnie died last night."

SAMANTHA

ut it out, Sam!"

Sounds as if someone is annoyed by whatever Sam is doing, doesn't it?

"Knock it off, Sam. Go back to Judy's room."

Sounds like mischief afoot. Or at least someone wants to get rid of Sam for a while.

"A feeling of utter calm, like a cool hand on one's forehead in the midst of acute terror; a pervasive gentleness." Also descriptive of Sam's effect on others, though contrasting. Like a warm blanket wrapped around them; a warm, good feeling.

Sam had come to be accepted by the family that lived in the large, two-story square house in a town in Jackson County. This family needed the spacious home more than did the previous occupants, who had inherited it from the original owner, a business man who built the house in the early 1900's. His wife had died in one of the four upstairs bedrooms. She was quite elderly by then and had been ill for some time.

(119)

When the current family bought the house in the late 1950's and settled in, the oldest daughter Peggy at age 11 took her pick of the bedrooms. Her choice was the northeast room. Her two younger sisters, six and four at the time, were told to take the room across the hall. That left a bedroom for their parents, a guest bedroom, a study, and a bathroom all on the second floor. And so, who would have which room was settled. For a while.

Elaine and Judy weren't happy with their room. They felt something strange about it, and they were frightened. They said it was way too cold, all the time, even though it was the beginning of summer when they moved in. Their room also seemed dark or crowded, to them. Elaine said later, " . . . like sitting in a chair recently vacated by someone else, the person's presence still lingering."

Then the noises started. At first, the family thought they were the normal sounds of an old house settling or the loud cracks sometimes heard when the outdoor temperatures drop fast.

"But eventually," Elaine said, "we all had to admit to hearing the measured thump of

feet on the stairs and the occasional clang of a pan being filled with water in the basement.

"As time passed," she continued, "I graduated to the room across the hall, leaving Judy in 'that room,' as we all referred to it. We were in our early teens, and though teenagers' perceptions of reality and fantasy can be questionable, they *do* and we *did* know the difference. We had taken to calling the presence Sam, short for Samantha. And she became most active during the years 1967 to 1974."

The girls' father told of the first really frightening experience the youngest daughter, Judy, had. "She woke up one night," he said, "feeling someone shaking her bed. She saw a woman standing there. She knew it wasn't her mother. She saw a fairly slender woman with long, light hair – a little wavy on the ends. She had large, dark eyes and seemed to be wearing a long, light – maybe white – dress. The woman stood there and looked at Judy. Judy felt afraid and started to say something, but the figure disappeared. After it was gone, Judy

(121)

wasn't afraid anymore. She felt unbelievably calm, considering."

Sam's appearance always happened when Judy was upset or concerned about something. When she felt Sam sit down on her bed, and she could see the bed "down" on that side but no one there, she was calmed by Sam's presence. When she stopped worrying about her problems, the "dip" came up again and all was normal.

Sometimes, Judy said, the presence actually touched her. Instantly she was calm and able to go to sleep again.

Elaine told about other happenings in their home. Some evenings the window shades all snapped up at the same time. Pictures fell off the wall in unison. The heavy furniture and marble-topped tables would be spun askew in the middle of the night.

Elaine remembers most vividly a night when she was 17, Judy was 15, and their parents had gone out for the evening. When the girls finally settled down to the business of getting to bed, the shade snapping and clattering and general noise started up in Judy's room. After a while, Elaine heard Judy say in a loud voice, "Knock it off, Sam. Go to Elaine's room."

A second later, Elaine felt the air in her room

move. Elaine recalled, "It was cooler and carried a scent of flowers. Nothing happened beyond that, and I eventually drifted off to sleep.

"I awoke hours later in the grip of the most acute terror I had ever felt. The edge of my bed dipped down as if someone had just sat down on it. I felt a cool hand on my forehead, followed by an almost liquid-like calmness. It was just as my sister had described it: cold terror, then something as soothing as warm water – a pervasive gentleness.

"I sometimes wondered if Sam's appearance left a door open for someone unpleasant, and Sam had to take care to remove that other presence.

"At any rate, I got used to feeling Sam's closeness, like another member of the family, almost. Sometimes I said, 'Sam, go back to Judy's room.' "

Judy told about her *most* frightening experience. It happened when she was in sixth or seventh grade. She was in her room, that same northwest room, one night. She woke up. Things didn't feel right. The room was very cold. Then she saw a man standing at the foot of her bed. He wore a tall, black hat and dark clothing, but he had no face. Judy had the inexplicable feeling that someone was extremely angry.

(123)

Then Samantha came, and the man disappeared. Again, it was as if Samantha took care to remove the unpleasant presence.

The girls' parents told of times when they smelled perfume. "Sam's identifying smell was pleasant, that of a woman busy in her home, cooking, cleaning, etc. This all made sense," Elaine told, "since we believe she is the spirit of the lady for whom the house was built, who raised her family there, and who died there, in that bedroom that was Judy's for so long."

There were many times when members of the family turned to take a second look at a shadow. But one summer, when Elaine was visiting friends in another state, her father walked down the upstairs hall late one night. As he went by Elaine's bedroom, he passed someone. He thought at first it was Elaine, but then realized she wasn't home. He quickly looked into her bedroom, but there was no one there.

Elaine claims that when Samantha is seen, "There isn't real substance or form, but rather a suggestion of shape, an impression of gender, a feeling. Apparently it is a similar impression to the one I leave. Dad thought he saw me that night he first saw Sam."

Guests of the family have experienced Sam, too. One young man who came to visit was put up overnight in the guest room because a blizzard had come up and delayed his leaving. In the morning, he said that someone had rattled the doorknob in the night.

He said he opened the door, but no one was there. Later he heard it rattle again. He got up real fast once and looked out in the hall. He heard someone walking down and up but couldn't see anyone. The young man never visited there again.

Another guest came to visit Judy one winter. Again, when it was time for him to leave, traveling was out of the question. He was put up in the guest room. Just after he went to bed, he felt something hit the bed. The bed went down. Then he felt pressure on his chest. He thought the family's fifteen-pound Manx cat had landed  on him. When he found out in the morning that the cat had been in the basement all night, he learned to accept Samantha as the ghost in the house, almost a member of the family.

One summer, the girls' father woke up to feel someone holding his right hand. It was a warm and soft grasp, but firm, too, like the palm of another hand, just clasping his. He thought, I must be dreaming. He looked at the wall to see shadows of tree branches with their leaves, moving in the light from the street as usual. He noticed that the window was open. He wasn't dreaming. Just as he tried to grab the hand to look at it, it slipped out of his hand and disappeared. He turned to see that his wife was sound asleep beside him. No one else was there in the room. He wasn't frightened, though. He said it was a comforting hand.

His wife's experiences are different. She'll suddenly smell something like a delicate fragrance. "It's pleasant," she said. "Sometimes I smell it when I wake up at night. It's there for a while. Then it's gone. I can't pin it to anything. It's not like the others' experiences."

If things disappear, "Sam's been here" is the explanation. Or if something shows up that wasn't there earlier, "Sam must have left it."

As in this case. The girls' mother had just finished a thorough housecleaning. A few days later, there was a piece of metal on one girl's bedroom floor. It appeared to be part of an old gun barrel, but there were no guns in the house. "And a piece of metal that size could never have escaped my mother's scrutiny," Elaine pointed out.

She also said that articles of clothing had disappeared over the years. Not one sock caught in the washer, but shirts, sets of lingerie, favorite jeans. Elaine said she thought maybe Sam's cleaning schedule didn't mesh with her mother's, and Sam just went on cleaning and straightening up on her own, when she was ready. Maybe she put their clothing in a special place, reserved for her own daughter. Or maybe she had decided to take over the mending.

At the end of one Christmas vacation, when Elaine was ready to go back to school, she and her mother looked and looked for one item of clothing that had been a gift. Elaine wanted to take it back with her. They took time out for lunch. When they went back up to Elaine's room, they both saw the gift in its box, set up on end as if on display in the middle of the floor.

"Oh! Sam again!"

When Elaine and Judy were in college at the same time but in two other states, they were still visited by Sam. Elaine, who had always been the most sensitive to Sam, would get the feeling from Sam that Judy wanted to talk to her. When Elaine called Judy then, Judy was surprised. "Why, no, but let's talk anyway," she told Elaine.

Each of the girls has been married for several years now. Elaine has a family and lives in a city in another state. Samantha seems to have followed her there.

In the new home, a key disappeared once, but it was found right where Elaine had looked, where she expected it to be, but it wasn't. Until Sam put it back.

Another time, Elaine came downstairs to the living room

(127)

to find the chair near the fireplace rocking. She knew then that Samantha had been there, too.

And Sam goes to yet another state to visit Judy, who still remembers her very cold room at home and the visits from Samantha.

Elaine wonders if Samantha will stay with the family through the current younger generation. Her two-year-old son has already met Sam. He left  his room several times one night when he couldn't get to sleep. The third or fourth time, Elaine asked, "What's happening? You ought to be asleep by now." He finally asked his mother to get "that lady" out of his room. Then Elaine told Sam to get out, and Sam moved on.

Elaine's husband has also met Sam. When he was talking on the phone one night, when Elaine was sound asleep, he heard someone ask, "Who's on the phone?" Puzzled, he didn't answer. He was asked again. The third time, he just blinked his eyes and the quizzing stopped. Immediately, Sam was gone.

Judy and Elaine have been aware of Samantha most of their lives and have believed in her. Elaine's personal note was, "We see her as capable of communicating emotion. She seems to be aware of our emotions. We consider ouselves lucky to have someone from another place and time know us and care about us."

NO PEACE FOR MORTALS

 ean and her husband woke up with a start. "What time is it?" she whispered. Just then the living room clock struck two.

"Did you hear something, too?" Al asked.

"Yes. Like a low moaning I thought I heard someone say 'I'm the man' or something like that."

Jean got up then and walked through the house, listening closely. When she passed the bathroom, she realized the sound was coming from there. It was the children's talking He-Man toothbrush set.

Al took out the batteries, and they both figured that would end the disturbance.

"But the next morning, about nine o'clock," Jean said, "I heard the sound again. It seemed to be coming from the toothbrush set, even without batteries. But it didn't sound like talking now. It was more of a low, garbled mumble, as if someone wasn't satisfied with the way things were.

"I threw it in the garbage then. It was just too scary.

"Late one night I was wakened by a baby crying. I got up and walked down the hall to the kids' room. They were asleep, and everything looked all right. But I missed something. The next day I was outside, and right by the steps I saw my son's night light. It was a little ceramic boy kneeling by a lamb, like a shepherd boy with his arm around his lamb . . . or like a 'Now I lay me down to sleep' figurine. It had been a gift at the birth of our son. But now the little boy's head was broken off.

"At the time, the kids were pretty young. One was still a baby. The other one was about three. I wondered what this was all about. It reminded me of Agatha Christie's *Ten Little Indians*. Was this broken night light a warning that something would happen to one of the family? Was it a ghost sending us a signal? And if it was, whose ghost?

"Even when I went back to bed, I could hear a baby crying. And we talked about it a lot. The only possibility we came up with was that the ghost might be connected with a relative's tragic death. The spouse survived, and a very young child suddenly had just one parent.

"The relative had spent the night on the farm with

(130)

us the night before the accident."

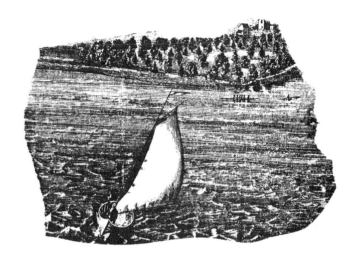

The next stange experience Jean told about seemed to support her theory. "A few weeks after the accident, our infant son's pacifier disappeared. He was really attached to that pacifier, and of course he cried a lot. We looked literally everywhere that night. Mom even came and helped us look. It wasn't anywhere around, though. Finally we quit looking for it, but the baby didn't quit crying. I think he cried half the night.

"The next morning, when we got up, the pacifier was lying on the floor right by the front door. We'd all looked there, too, and even outside the door!"

Could it be that, as a result of the sudden, tragic accident and death, the ghost could find no peace and didn't want the relatives to have peace, either? Not even the baby, with the comfort of his pacifier? When that thought was verbalized, relatives recall-that pacifiers had not been an accepted way to comfort a baby in the victim's way of thinking. Or maybe the absent one was missing the child who had just celebrated a first birthday that month and in the future would celebrate her birthdays without one parent. Or perhaps the one who had always been young in spirit before the accident just didn't want to depart this life at such an early age.

Jean finished her story with the report that these incidents have never happened when guests have been around. "The ghost appears only to the family, but not in visible form. More through actions performed by the invisible member of the family.

"But when family members come to visit the farm where we live and where my family grew up, they have a strange, haunting feeling whenever they walk near it or come on the place. As if none of us will ever be allowed to forget."

WEIRD SOUNDS AND WINDMILLS

dell Barnes, who lives on a farm in Murray County, was frightened by daytime sounds of someone going up to second floor bedrooms. From her bed at night, she heard someone running fast from the north room into the landing which was used as a daughter's bedroom. Then she heard it run into the couples' own bedroom and out through the wall.

One night something walked alongside the bed on Adell's side and then seemed to move through the wall to the outside.

She said, "The kids never heard anything. Neither did my husband."

When someone asked Adell if she ever saw anything, she said, "No. I was so afraid, I wouldn't open my eyes to look. And I never felt anything either. I just heard the sounds."

At that time, Adell and Charlie had been sleeping upstairs. They decided to move their bedroom down to what had been a dining room. Charlie

(133)

helped take the bedroom furniture down and Adell rearranged the clothing and made up the bed again.

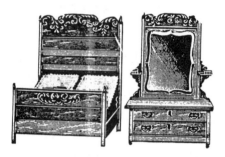

One night when they were asleep, Adell sensed someone walking across the foot of the bed, across her feet, back and forth.

They didn't have a cat or a dog so it had to be something other than a household pet. She didn't look, but she woke up wide and she is sure she had felt the motion. She tried to be brave. She told herself, "Now, this is silly. There's nothing in here going across the foot of the bed."

Just then, she felt something like a hot breath or breeze blowing into her face. She stayed there, frozen in fear, and pulled the covers over her head.

Maybe these incidents had such a terrifying effect on Adell because of an earlier experience. When she was a girl of thirteen or fourteen, she and her older sister Bonita stayed home one night on the family's farm in Murray County. Their parents had gone to a dance and wouldn't be back until late because refreshments were always served after the dance, at the home of the hosts. Usually they had cake and coffee.

As they left, Adell's father said, "Now, you both know you have to turn the windmill off after it has pumped long enough. Take care of it before you go to bed, and don't forget." Fred could be real stern.

About an hour later, the girls went out to shut the windmill off. Back in the house, they had a glass of milk and some soft molasses cookies and went upstairs to get ready for bed.

(135)

Through the open window, they could hear the pump start up again. Pulling overalls over their  nighties, they went down again to see if they hadn't secured the handle that shut the windmill off. They knew that when they pulled the lever down, they had to fasten it securely with the heavy wire to the corner support of the windmill frame.

"Maybe we didn't fasten it well enough before," Bonita said as they made sure it was secured this time.

Having had enough of running back and forth in the increasing darkness, they went right up to bed. By now it was at least ten o'clock. The pump started working again, and it was an eerie sound. The wheel at the top of the windmill creaked as it slowly started around. Then the blades howled. Exasperated, Adell said, "I'm not going out there again!" And they went to bed and soon fell asleep.

When their parents got home about 1:30 from the dance, the windmill was still going. Fred went out to check it and found it wasn't shut off.

(136)

Naturally, the girls were in for a scolding the next morning. But after they told their father they had secured the lever twice, he was thoughtful and quiet for a while. Then he told them maybe it wasn't their fault, but he wouldn't explain.

Years later, while Adell and Charlie lived on this same place, they were out milking in the barn one evening. They had four children at that time, and Adell, the young mother, was 29 or 30. As Adell carried the milk to the cooler, a thought came through to her, as if someone said, "Your Dad isn't going to be with you much longer." There was no one there, and she heard no real voice. "But the thought came into my mind," she said.

Adell knew her father had been in the hospital earlier, but he'd been discharged with a clean bill of health.

Adell told Charlie, "Grandpa was 85 when he died. Dad has a long time to live yet." But her father died on December 29, just a couple months after the warning.

Her father seemed to have a premonition, too, that he would die soon. He said to Adell, "Some day you're going to have to take care of Mom."

One morning at breakfast, Fred and his wife looked again at all their Christmas cards and shared fudge and coffee. Then he went out to the garage to leave for work.

He usually left the garage door open when he went to work. His wife saw later that day that the garage door was shut. When she noticed it, she didn't recall having heard it opening that morning. When she and the neighbors checked, they found Fred dead of a heart attack.

CONTENTS OF A BOX

hen Donna and Bill Wentworth moved to a house in rural Nobles County, they noticed something strange. There were no doors between the living room and dining room. That in itself wasn't unusual. They knew that many homes have a wide, open archway or a simple wide space in the wall between those rooms. But they noticed it was always cold there. Someone told Donna that an unexplainable cold area in a house indicated that it was haunted, and the cold spot was the place where the ghost came and went.

Sometimes they felt a sensation as of the wind blowing their hair there, a little like the way a fan in the entrance to a church will blow it on a hot Sunday morning in July. But you can see the fan and try to dodge it. Here there was no fan. Many times when the Wentworths were in that place, they felt activity or energy of some kind causing movement of air; yet there was nothing like a motor or fan turning.

Sometimes in mild weather, Donna came in

through the back door of the house. As soon as she stepped into the kitchen, she would hear voices. Often as many as five or six men seemed to be talking in the living room. Their voices were jumbled, and she wasn't able to sort out any one voice or figure out what was being said. The sound resembled that of a radio when the station isn't tuned in well. She often went into the living room to turn the radio off, only to find that it wasn't on.

One day someone who had lived in the house earlier came back to visit. When he was told about the voices, he explained them with one comment: "Oh! The card games in the parlor!" But that's all he would say.

Aside from the voices, a few more things happened. When Donna and Bill had lived there a couple years, Donna decided it was time to clean out the attic. She was curious as to what was up there. When she had gone in through the small door, she screwed an adapter into a socket and connected an extension cord and a crookneck lamp. All set, she was ready to explore the attic. Suddenly the door slammed shut, the extension cord came out of the socket, and she sat on the attic floor in total darkness. No explanation seemed plausible.

Another time, Donna had just gotten up in the

morning when, before she went anywhere near the kitchen, she could hear water running there.

Going to check on it, she found the faucet completely open and water gushing full force into the sink. It took two or three turns to turn it off. She's still wondering how it got turned on.

One day when she sat alone in a rocking chair in the dining room, she heard the steps creak, one by one, as they would if someone were coming down from upstairs. She could see the door at the bottom of the stairway, and she watched it. After waiting for what must have been at least ten minutes and feeling more frightened by the minute, she got up, jerked open the door, and found . . . nothing there!

Another ghostly incident was a visual happening, in winter, with snow on the ground. There were footprints in the snow, and they came to the back porch. They were neither Donna's nor Bill's. There were definite tracks, though, as of someone who

walked up to the back door and never left. The size of the prints was normal, a medium size. If they were made by an overshoe, the soles were worn smooth. There was no snow inside on the floors, melted or other-wise. There was just the one short path, starting in the middle of the back yard and continuing to the back door. And no backtracking in the same prints so as to make them confusing. No one had gone in. The Wentworths weren't even using that door at the time; it was secured and weatherproofed for winter. Would a ghost suddenly appear out of nowhere and then leave footprints in the snow?

When the couple first moved to that house, several other families had lived there before them. Each family upon moving out had taken all their possessions with them. But one day, Donna noticed something she had never seen before. The closet under the stairway to the second floor had an overhead shelf just above the door space. She hadn't noticed it before, and neither had her husband. The shelf was just a little above head height, and not in the direct line of vision as they entered the closet and looked straight ahead. That day, though, Donna noticed it and got a stepstool so she could reach the shelf.

She found a flower box. The printing at the end of the box indicated it came from Ludlow Greenhouses, an early business in Worthington. Donna read, "LUDLOW GREENHOUSES...LUDLOW BROS., PROPS. FLORAL DESIGNS A SPECIALTY. DELIVER WITHOUT DELAY."

Donna and Bill found out that Ludlow Bros. Greenhouses had operated from about 1916 to early in 1944. Milton, the oldest of the Ludlow brothers, and H. Dwight, the youngest, were the owners. The other brother, J. Burr Ludlow, was a banker and insurance man. Helen Wilson Smith remembers when the men made steel frames for the glass for the structure that housed all the plants. Smith, still a resident of the area, knew five generations of the Ludlow family. But the business had been sold to a Sioux Falls firm.

That didn't help explain anything except where the box had originally come from. Still curious, Donna took it to a table near a window where the light was better. In the box were various objects, and she took them out one by one, thinking mementos . . . or maybe souvenirs. If mementos, she thought to herself, they were meant to either warn or remind. If souvenirs, they were merely remembrances, objects saved as a pleasant reminder of days gone by. Among other things, she lifted out a violin, a man's Gillette razor,

a bundle of letters, and a wool vest. The razor was in its original package as if ready for a first shave whenever needed. What seemed hard to believe was that all those other people had lived in the house and no one had removed the box or the items in it. Not sure what to do with it, she put the box back on the shelf.

Thinking about the shiny, new razor, Donna started to remember something. She had been told when they moved in that one of the earliest families to live in the house had a sad experience. A son had died at a very young age, either in the house or in a hospital while the house was his home. In fact, the time connected with his death would fit into the time span the Ludlows operated in Worthington. Now, what do I do with these things, she wondered. Were they his?

A long time later, two men came to the Wentworths' door. One of them asked, "Could we see the house and farm? This is where we grew up, as did our younger brother. But he got real sick while we all lived here, and he died before we moved away."

Donna invited them in. In the course of the conversation, she ventured, "There's something funny here, though. Something rather unsettling. Did you notice anything strange about the place when you lived here?"

They both said they hadn't. And it seemed that they didn't want to talk about that any more. They just wanted to see the place. Then they slowly made the rounds of the house and yard, coming again to the porch to say, "Thank you for letting us come. And you won't be bothered anymore."

And they weren't. Nothing else happened like the earlier events. And the brothers didn't come back. It was as if, in coming that one time, they had released the spirit of their brother who had died young. It seems he had stuck around, doing nothing destructive, but just hanging around as if he wasn't ready to leave his home and his treasured possessions when he died.

"And one more detail," Donna added. "The next time I hung my jacket in that stairway closet, the flower box was gone!"

(144)

A FRIENDLY GHOST

 ucille was saying, "Oh, Bob, I think I just *have* to have it."

And Bob's answer was a question. "Are you sure you want more old junk around?"

This conversation took place before Bob got hooked on collectibles. Lucille had been into them for quite a while already, in the days when there would be only three or four rummage sale ads in the paper at a time.

At this particular sale, Lucille fell in love with an old rocking chair. It seemed to greet her with a built-in personality. It looked as if it would be comfortable, with its back and seat upholstered and its sides open. Because it was also a pretty chair, it was a bargain at $2.50.

Lucille won out, and Bob resignedly helped her haul the chair home.

(145)

They tried it downstairs at first. It *was* comfortable. And, despite its age, if they just pushed it to make it rock, it didn't squeak. But if they *sat* in it and rocked, it squeaked. The family came to think of it as a nice squeak as if a friend was always there visiting and rocking. Since it became so close and important, Bob began to refer to it as THE CHAIR, with emphasis when he spoke of it.

But as more "old junk" found its way into the rooms on the main floor, Bob suggested THE CHAIR be taken up to the attic. Something had to go. There wasn't room to move around anymore, and their eight children needed a little space to play and grow.

At that time, the family all slept upstairs in their home on Nobles Street in Worthington. Kelly, the youngest daughter, was thirteen or fourteen. Her room was the first one at the top of the stairs. In the far corner of her room is a door to the attic. By tugging a little on that door, one can open it and climb several steps up to the space filled with boxes of high school souvenirs, old chairs, love seats, and other memorabilia. With them, THE CHAIR took up residence.

Kasey, Kelly's young brother, was about three when Kelly was about thirteen. No one knew that there was any connection with a mystery about the house, but Kasey let it be known that he would rather crawl in with Kelly in her big bed than sleep alone in his room.

One night, and *only* one night, Kelly heard the neat chair rocking in the attic. *And* squeaking. She knew that meant someone was sitting in it, but no one had gone through her room and opened the door to the attic. At least, she hadn't seen or heard anyone. As scared as she was, she couldn't make herself get up to check. Petrified, she was happy to have Kasey with her that night. She stayed in bed and eventually went back to sleep.

Before that, Lucille herself had gone up to the attic one day and had seen the chair rocking. It was squeaking, too. Yet no one visible was sitting in it, and no attic windows were open to cause a draft that would start it rocking. After that day, Lucille never wanted to open the door to the attic stairs, unless there was a support team present.

After Bob began to get interested in collectibles, too, the doorbell rang one Saturday morning. At first, Bob thought someone had come to see a particular item or just to look around. By now, he thought he knew enough about the business to take care of a customer. Three of the girls were home that morning, but Bob beat them to the door. A man and woman stood there on the steps.

The man said, "I used to live here in this house years ago." Further talk led to "While I lived here, my little brother died when he was eight. He died in one of the upstairs rooms."

It turned out to be Kasey's room, not Kelly's. One of the girls asked the visitor, "Would that explain why Kasey doesn't like to sleep in his room alone?"

The man's only answer was that he'd sure like to come in and have a look around, if they didn't mind.

The girls took him and his companion all through the house, downstairs and upstairs and even through the porches, where some of the collectibles were displayed on the shelves. He seemed to enjoy the tour and their chatter about a ghost. The kids had all talked about it for a long time. Lucille didn't encourage that kind of talk, but she didn't stifle it either. By then the family had accepted the ghost in their home even though they hadn't figured out why it was there.

Before the visitors left, Lucille said, "It was nice to talk with you. I'm glad you were able to come and see the home you used to live in. That must be a good feeling, to be able to do that."

The visitor agreed, and he thanked them for the tour. Before he left, he told them that he was sure they had a nice, friendly ghost and they shouldn't be afraid of it. He said he thought the ghost felt at home there, and since they had accepted it, they would have no problems because of it.

"In fact," he said, "I wonder if it is maybe the ghost of my little brother."

THE GHOST OF DEADMAN'S HILL

 he ghost of Deadman's Hill is known by those who live in the vicinity of a farm north of Willmar. The incident that initiated the story happened on Alice's parents' home place.

Alice first heard of the ghost as a young girl in the summer of 1937, when an elderly neighbor came to help turn the hay that a two-day rain had soaked.

That noon, the neighbor whom the family called "old Joe" surprised Alice and her brother. When Alice spread a rug in the shade of the big American elm tree and invited "old Joe" to sit down and rest until her mother had lunch ready, he protested. He said, "No one should sit on a grave. Please be so kind as to move the rug."

Alice felt humbled as she moved the rug to the shade of a smaller tree. That was when her brother asked, "But whose grave is under the elm tree?"

The answer to his question was the beginning of a long story. There is only room for a part of it here, though the rest is begging to be told.

Briefly, the American elm was planted as a living memorial to a runaway slave who was caught by a bounty hunter. The slave was chained to a fencepost for the night, but he managed to pull the post out of the ground and free of the fence. Apparently he crept up on the bounty hunter and the two fought it out. The slave beheaded his captor with the bounty hunter's own sword.

As a young boy before the Civil War, "old Joe" had accompanied his father to the same farm north of Willmar on the morning the body of a black man was found near a corner of the front porch. The man had suffered many gashes and was chained to a large log fence post. When the men followed his trail by the blood and the marks left by the post as it was dragged along, they found the body of a second man -- a white man – the bounty hunter.

The slave was buried where he died, near the corner of the porch on the farm, where the tree was later planted. The bounty hunter was buried on the hill nearby, where his body had been found.

Two more men died soon afterward, on the hill. One was the sharecropper who lived on the hill farm. The other was the caretaker who had consequently been asked to do the chores for the sharecropper's widow. By then, by the tracks in the snow, it had been figured out that the ghost of the runaway slave had attacked and beheaded the caretaker and the sharecropper in much the same way as the bounty hunter had been killed.

The three deaths that occurred on the hill were soon generally blamed on the ghost of the runaway slave, who became known as the ghost of Deadman's Hill.

Alice and her brother began to piece things together after "old Joe" told them the story of the ghost. They learned that their mother knew their house was haunted. She never heard the sounds, because she was deaf; but she claimed to have seen and sensed spirits in the house. And items like flatware and coffee cups and frying pans turned up missing. A day or so later, they were returned. Alice and her brother tried to convince their father that there were ghosts that took the items, but

(153)

he made it known that he held his children responsible.

One night, the two children stayed awake to listen for the ghost. What they heard that night, and every night after that if they stayed awake to listen, sent shivers up their spines. First they heard a faint continuous noise coming from the north and gradually getting louder and closer until it was right outside the dining room window. The sound was like that of an object being dragged on the ground. After it stopped just outside the window, they would hear the sound of chains clinking, then silence for about one minute before they heard more clinking.

The dragging sound would start again until it came to a sudden halt just past the corner of the house. The sound never varied, and it always occurred at the same time each night. "We could have set our clocks by it," Alice claimed. "We talked Dad  into listening to the ghost sounds with us several times, but he always claimed the sounds were caused by mice or rats between the walls, or the wind, or something else -- never a ghost!

"After World War II ended and building material became available again," Alice continued, "Dad bought windows, insulation, and siding to redo the downstairs of the oldest part of the house. My brother and I talked about the ghost during the time we were working on the house. Being older then, we knew that although there had been activity on the farm attributed to the Underground Railway, we would never actually find a tunnel,

so we had quit looking for it. But we decided that if during the remodeling we heard the same sounds we had been hearing, and if we still heard them *after* the remodeling was done, there *had* to be a ghost, not just the wind or something between the walls.

"Needless to say, the ghost of Deadman's Hill continued to make his nightly pilgrimage to the grave."

Alice clearly recalls one incident of a couple years later when she was twelve. It was a hot summer night in early August. She and her parents and brother had worked late in the field, shocking grain until it was too dark to see, before they headed home to start chores.

"I lit the kerosene lamp in the kitchen," Alice remembered. "We all had a bite to eat. Then the folks left for the barn to start the milking, taking with them the one lantern that had some kerosene in it.

"Meanwhile, I went to the shed for a can of kerosene to refill the house lamp and another lantern before joining the folks in the barn. By then it was pitch dark.

"As I started across the yard towards the shed, the night had not cooled off any. When I reached the shed, I felt my way along the row of gas barrels until I felt the smaller kerosene barrel on the far end of the row.

"After filling the can and feeling my way out of the shed, I faced toward the house. The light in the kitchen window was very dim. I didn't give this any significance at the time because I knew the lamp was almost empty and I thought it was just going out. It did make it harder to find my way.

"As I lost sight of the light entirely, there was no alternative so I kept walking toward the house. Very suddenly the air around me changed from hot to muggy to icy cold. The only thing I can think of to compare the change of temperature with is that it was like walking into the frozen food locker on a hot day.

"I hurried my steps, and in seconds the air was warm and muggy again. Much to my surprise, the lamp I thought had gone out was still burning.

"As I entered the house, my brother asked me if I heard the ghost go by. It wasn't until he mentioned the ghost that I looked at the time and realized I had crossed the ghost's path as he rested.

"Together, my brother and I listened as the ghost of Deadman's Hill once again finished his nightly journey to his grave."

EPILOGUE

Sometimes strange things happen and there is no ready explanation.

For example, think back ten or fifteen years to when Larson Crane Service of Worthington tore down a gas station and two old houses to clear the site for the new Worthington Federal Savings and Loan. A small child's tombstone was found in the wall of one house. It bore a name and a date. Yet excavations that followed brought no further explanation as to why the marker was located between walls, several feet up from the floor.

In 1938, a man had his two nephews working for him. In the smaller house where they stayed, the nephews heard a strange noise in the kitchen at a certain time every night. When they persuaded their uncle to sit in the kitchen with them and listen for the sound, it was on schedule. He looked around and discovered that the dipper in the water pail had a tiny hole in it. When the dipper filled itself with water, it sank to the bottom of the pail. That occurrence could be explained, and it was solved by the purchase of a new dipper.

In 1940, a woman died in her home. Since her brother's death fifteen years earlier, she had only left twice, to go to town. She did not want to be gone when her long-dead relatives "came to visit," so she lived out her last years alone in her home.

While I was gathering these stories, my husband and I drove through Peculiar, Missouri on our way home from a short vacation. Peculiar. That *is* the name of the town, and it *is* on the map.

Peculiar. I reached for the dictionary. I thought, That's what some of these stories are. Peculiar. Odd, curious, singular. Strange. Unusual.

You may be trying to figure them out as you read, just as I did as I wrote. Could they have happened? Who might the ghosts have been? Whose past do they represent? Why are they here?

NEED A GIFT?
For

- **Shower** • **Birthday** •
• **Mother's Day** • **Father's Day** •
• **Anniversary** • **Christmas** •
• **Graduation** • **Going Away** •

Turn Page For Order Form
(Order Now While Supply Lasts)

TO ORDER COPIES OF

GHOSTLY TALES OF SOUTHWEST MINNESOTA

Please send me_____copies of **Ghostly Tales of Southwest Minnesota** at $9.95 each. (Make checks payable to **QUIXOTE PRESS**.)

Name _____

Street _____

City _____ State _____ Zip Code ____

SEND ORDERS TO:
QUIXOTE PRESS
R.R. #4, Box 33B
Blvd. Station
Sioux City, Iowa 51109

TO ORDER COPIES OF

GHOSTLY TALES OF SOUTHWEST MINNESOTA

Please send me_____copies of **Ghostly Tales of Southwest Minnesota** at $9.95 each. (Make checks payable to **QUIXOTE PRESS**.)

Name _____

Street _____

City _____ State _____ Zip Code ____

SEND ORDERS TO:
QUIXOTE PRESS
R.R. #4, Box 33B
Blvd. Station
Sioux City, Iowa 51109

If you have enjoyed this book,
perhaps you would enjoy others
from Quixote Press.

GHOSTS OF THE MISSISSIPPI RIVER
Minneapolis to Dubuque by Bruce Carlson .paperback $9.95

GHOSTS OF THE MISSISSIPPI RIVER
Dubuque to Keokuk by Bruce Carlson . . . . . paperback $9.95

GHOSTS OF THE MISSISSIPPI RIVER
Keokuk to St. Louis by Bruce Carlson . . . . . paperback $9.95

GHOSTS OF JOHNSON COUNTY, IOWA
by Lori Erickson . . . . hardback $12.95

GHOSTS OF LINN COUNTY, IOWA
by Lori Erickson . . . . hardback $12.95

GHOSTS OF LEE COUNTY, IOWA
by Bruce Carlson . . . . hardback $12.00

GHOSTS OF DES MOINES COUNTY, IOWA
by Bruce Carlson . . . . hardback $12.00

GHOSTS OF SCOTT COUNTY, IOWA
by Bruce Carlson . . . . hardback $12.95

GHOSTS OF ROCK ISLAND COUNTY, ILLINOIS
by Bruce Carlson . . . . hardback $12.95

GHOSTS OF THE AMANA COLONIES
by Lori Erickson . . . . paperback $9.95

GHOSTLY TALES OF NORTHEAST IOWA
by Ruth Hein and Vicky Hinsenbrock . . . . . paperback $9.95

GHOSTS OF POLK COUNTY, IOWA
by Tom Welch . . . . paperback $9.95

GHOSTS OF THE IOWA GREAT LAKES
by Bruce Carlson . . . . paperback $9.95

MISSISSIPPI RIVER PO' FOLK
by Pat Wallace . . . . paperback $9.95

(163)

STRANGE FOLKS ALONG THE MISSISSIPPI
by Pat Wallace . . . . paperback $9.95

THE VANISHING OUTHOUSE OF IOWA
by Bruce Carlson . . . . paperback $9.95

THE VANISHING OUTHOUSE OF ILLINOIS
by Bruce Carlson . . . . paperback $9.95

THE VANISHING OUTHOUSE OF MINNESOTA
by Bruce Carlson . . . . paperback $9.95

THE VANISHING OUTHOUSE OF WISCONSIN
by Bruce Carlson . . . . paperback $9.95

MISSISSIPPI RIVER COOKIN' BOOK
by Bruce Carlson . . . . paperback $11.95

IOWA'S ROAD KILL COOKBOOK
by Bruce Carlson . . . . paperback $7.95

HITCH HIKING THE UPPER MIDWEST
by Bruce Carlson . . . . paperback $7.95

IOWA, THE LAND BETWEEN THE VOWELS
by Bruce Carlson . . . . paperback $9.95

GHOSTLY TALES OF SOUTHWEST MINNESOTA
by Ruth Hein . . . . paperback $9.95

GHOSTS ON THE COAST OF MAINE
by C. Schultz . . . . paperback $9.95

ME 'N WESLEY
by Bruce Carlson . . . . paperback $9.95

INDEX

(Titles of stories in this book are in capital letters. Towns are in Minnesota unless otherwise indicated.)

(169)

(173)